aloha lagoon

www.alohalagoonmysteries.com

D1398613

ALOHA LAGOON MYSTERIES

Ukulele Murder
Murder on the Aloha Express
Deadly Wipeout
Deadly Bubbles in the Wine
Mele Kalikimaka Murder
Death of the Big Kahuna
Ukulele Deadly
Bikinis & Bloodshed
Death of the Kona Man
Lethal Tide
Beachboy Murder
Handbags & Homicide
Tiaras & Terror

BOOKS BY ANNE MARIE STODDARD

Aloha Lagoon Mysteries:
Bikinis & Bloodshed
Handbags & Homicide
Tiaras & Terror

Amelia Grace Rock 'n' Roll Mysteries:
Murder at Castle Rock
"Caper at Castle Rock"
(short story in the Killer Beach Reads collection)
Deception at Castle Rock
"Sleighed at Castle Rock"
(holiday short story)

HANDBAGS & HOMICIDE

an Aloha Lagoon mystery

Anne Marie Stoddard

This book is for the wonderful women of my own bridal party: Allison, Liz, Claire, Stella, Kathleen, Becky, Aubrey, & Camila. Love you all!

ACKNOWLEDGEMENTS

First and foremost, I'd like to thank Gemma Halliday for her guidance and support. I'm grateful to work with such an incredible author and mentor! I'd also like to thank the Gemma Halliday Publishing team for helping give my stories some much-needed polish—especially Susan and Jenny for their work on this book. A shout out is also due to my husband, Eric, for his patience while I locked myself away to hammer out another one of Kaley's adventures. I also want to thank Kristin Burks for helping name the Lanai Lounge, a new setting featured in this book. And finally, I want to thank anyone who picks up this book for giving my writing a chance. I hope you enjoy reading it as much as I enjoyed writing it.

"Best of all, at the end of your creative adventure, you have a souvenir--something you MADE, something to remind you forever of your brief but transformative encounter with inspiration. That's what my books are to me: souvenirs of journeys that I took, in which I managed (blessedly) to escape myself for a little while." —Elizabeth Gilbert, *Big Magic*

CHAPTER ONE

―――――

"*I'm getting married!*" my friend from Atlanta, Emma Ross, gushed. She let out a squeal so loud that I almost had to pull the phone away from my ear. "Kaley, isn't it so exciting?"

When Emma had sent me a *"9-1-1"* text message five minutes earlier, I'd bolted off the sales floor of the Happy Hula Dress Boutique, the clothing shop I managed at the Aloha Lagoon Resort, without a moment's hesitation. I had hurried into the office that I shared with my Aunt Rikki, worried that something horrible had happened to my dear friend. A break-up, a lost job—or maybe a really bad spray tan. I certainly hadn't expected *this*.

"That's great, Em," I said, wincing at the shrillness of her voice. "Congratulations." I quickly crossed the office and pulled the door closed, hoping that my friend's ecstatic squealing hadn't been heard from the sales floor. Then I returned to the desk and sank into the cushioned chair. "When's the wedding?" I asked, my own voice coming out a half-octave higher than usual. While I was happy for Emma, the engagement seemed rather sudden. She had only been dating Atlanta Falcons' star defensive end, Dante Becker, for just over four months.

"Well…" Emma's tone was a little reluctant now. "That's part of the reason I'm calling. Obviously, I wanted to tell you right after Dante popped the question." There was a pause, and she sighed with contentment. I pictured my petite brunette friend on the other end of the line, marveling at a massive diamond on her left ring finger. "Anyway," she continued, "we didn't want to wait until next year, and with football season right around the corner, Dante's about to be busy twenty-four-seven. You know how it is."

"Yeah." I pursed my lips. I did know. Until recently I'd been a football wife myself. My ex-husband, Bryan Colfax, was Dante's teammate. We'd actually been the ones to introduce the newly engaged couple. Of course, that was before my NFL star hubby had cheated on me with three of the team's new cheerleaders (one of which happened to be Dante's cousin)—all at the same time. We'd divorced nearly two months ago, and the last I'd heard, Bryan was dating one of those home-wrecking pompom shakers. *Good riddance.* I scowled at the memory.

"So, anyway, we're going to do it a week from next Tuesday," Emma blurted, bringing my attention back to her.

I nearly dropped the phone. "For real?" Today was Thursday, which put the ceremony less than two weeks away. It was also currently the middle of July. The team's preseason would start in mid-August, and the guys were already training daily. "Em, that's not enough time to plan a wedding. How are you going to book a venue within that kind of window? What about a dress? And a honeymoon? Can Dante even manage to take off around the team's practice schedule?"

"Oh, don't worry. We've got it all handled," my friend replied smoothly. "We're getting married on a Tuesday morning so that Dante's schedule isn't interrupted. We're just having a small ceremony with family and close friends. Besides, Dante is still recovering from his knee surgery last month, so he's been spending most of practice on the bench. It's not like he'll miss much. We'll be taking a late honeymoon to Fiji—we just have to wait to see how the Falcons do postseason before we book the trip. Plus I pulled some strings with my yoga instructor's girlfriend, who works at that exclusive boutique in Buckhead, Bella's Bridal. I have an appointment tomorrow to try on dresses." She sighed again. "I wish you could go with me."

"Me too." I felt a pang of sorrow. I missed Emma so much. I wanted to be there for every step leading up to her big day, but I was across the continent in Hawaii, and it was such short notice. "Are you sure you're not rushing into this?" I asked gently. "Why not wait until the postseason? That would give you more time to plan, and maybe I could come visit and help you—
"

"We're in *love*," Emma interrupted, sounding defensive. "We don't wanna wait until the postseason." She sniffed. "I thought you'd be happy for me."

"Oh, sweetie." I smacked my palm to my forehead. I hadn't meant to upset her. "Of course I am."

"Good," Emma said, the perkiness returning to her voice. "Because I want you to be my maid of honor."

"Really?" It was my turn to squeal with excitement. "Em, I'd *love* to!" About two seconds later, the rational side of my brain caught up, and my pleasure was replaced by panic. Emma wanted me to help her plan a wedding that was just twelve days away. I chewed my lip, thinking of my barren bank account. Even if I worked on my days off for the next couple of weeks, the round-trip flight from Kauai to Atlanta would nearly drain my savings.

As if she'd read my mind, Emma piped up. "I was hoping you'd say yes—because Dante and I want to pay for your plane ticket back to Atlanta. How does first class sound?"

My jaw dropped open. "Em, that's such a generous offer," I breathed. "But you don't have to do that." I'd find a way to pay for a ticket myself. Maybe I could ask Aunt Rikki for an advance on my next paycheck.

"I know we don't have to, but we insist," she said. "And don't you dare start talking about paying us back. We want you to be there, and this is the least we can do. You did set us up, after all. We owe you."

"Girl, you don't owe me a thing. But seriously, thank you," I added softly, feeling a rush of gratitude.

"That reminds me," Emma said. "I wanted to find out who you're bringing for a plus one. Still seeing that hottie you told me about? If you'll send me his info, I'll book his flight, too. What was his name again?"

"Noa." I felt my insides warm at the thought of my childhood best bud—and, as of a few weeks ago, more than just a friend—Noa Kahele. "I'll talk to him about it tonight at dinner, though I'm sure he'll insist on paying for himself." Noa ran his own freelance business as a website and graphic designer. He was really good at his job, and business had been booming lately. Though he didn't need the supplemental income, he worked part-time as a lifeguard at the Aloha Lagoon Resort. Noa was usually stationed at the guest swimming pool right across the courtyard from Happy Hula, which meant I got the occasional glimpse of him in action through the shop's display window. I wasn't embarrassed to admit that it was the highlight of my shift on those days. He was usually shirtless when he worked at the pool, and the man rocked a *nice* set of abs.

A knock on the office door made me jump. "Hang on just a sec, Em," I said, rising from the desk chair.

"Wait!" she squawked. "Just one more thing, and then I'll let you go. It's almost dinnertime here, anyway, and Dante and I have reservations at Bacchanalia."

"Okay," I relented, swiveling in the chair. "Just a minute!" I called toward the closed office door.

Emma cleared her throat. "Since you're the maid of honor, I'm sure you're wondering how to go about hosting a bridal shower and bachelorette party on such short notice."

I felt the blood drain from my face. Neither of those things had even occurred to me yet. Unless she wanted a quick, *super* cheap celebration the day before the wedding, I wasn't sure there was any way I could pull it off—especially with less than two weeks to go until the big day.

"Well, you don't need to worry yourself about a shower. Dante's mother is handling that this Saturday."

"And the bachelorette party?" I asked, fighting to keep the panic out of my voice.

"Is next weekend." Emma giggled. "In Hawaii. I knew you wouldn't be able to fly home for the ceremony *and* the bachelorette festivities, so we're bringing the party to you. Surprise!"

My eyes went wide. "Are you serious?"

"As a heart attack, honey." I could practically hear Emma grinning. "You know I don't joke about a good party. I've already booked a couple of rooms at the Aloha Lagoon Resort for next weekend. I just need you to plan a few fun activities for us to do while we're there. Dante's offered to pick up the tab for everything, so just let me know how much everything will cost, and I'll run it by him and send over his card info. We'll arrive on Thursday afternoon, and then you and that sexy surfer man of yours can fly back to Atlanta with us on Sunday to get ready for the ceremony."

"That sounds great." I did a little dance in my chair. I was going to see Emma in just over a week, right here in Kauai!

"Oh, and feel free to invite any of your other gal pals from the island to join us for the weekend," Emma replied. "I'm only bringing the other bridesmaids, so the more the merrier."

"Who are your other bridesmaids?" I asked.

Emma coughed. "Oh, you know—just some of the football girlfriends," she said quickly. I thought I detected something in her tone that resembled reluctance—or worry, maybe?—but it was gone a moment later. "Anyway, I've gotta run," she said. "Dante hates being late for dinner reservations. I'll send over our flight and room info tomorrow." She squealed. "I can't wait to see you! This is gonna be so much fun. Later, tater."

I was still buzzing from Emma's exciting news as I slipped my phone back into the pocket of my peach-colored tube dress and got up to open the office door. My new pal and coworker, Jamie Parker, stood on the other side, her thin, blonde eyebrows raised in curiosity.

"Everything okay? I was walking past the office on the way back from the stock room and thought I heard screaming." Her lips twitched. "It sounded like you were murdering a pixie," she added in an accent similar to Emma's Georgia lilt.

I had a feeling my two friends would hit it off when they met face-to-face next weekend. Jamie had grown up in the South before moving to Aloha Lagoon to be the resort scuba diving instructor, which is what she did when she wasn't working cashier shifts at Happy Hula.

"No pixies," I said with a laugh. "I was on the phone with Emma, my closest friend back in Atlanta. She dropped a pretty big bombshell on me."

Jamie glanced over her shoulder, down the hallway that led to the boutique's sales floor. "It's pretty slow out there. Harmony and Rose can handle it for a few minutes." She stepped into the office and closed the door behind her. "What kind of bombshell?" she asked, giving me her full attention.

"She's getting married."

Jamie opened her mouth to cheer, her face alight with excitement, but I held up a finger to stop her.

"A week from next Tuesday," I finished.

Her grin vanished. "Whoa," she breathed. Her forehead wrinkled. "What's the rush? Does she have a bun in the oven?"

I shook my head. "No, nothing like that." I explained the limited time window in Dante's schedule with football season fast approaching. "They want to have the ceremony before the preseason kicks off, and they'll delay their honeymoon until after the playoffs." I sat back down in my desk chair. "She's flying me to Atlanta for the wedding, but first she and her other bridesmaids are coming to Aloha Lagoon next weekend for the bachelorette party. They'll be here a week from today." I glanced at the calendar on the wall. "That means I've got less than seven days to plan the perfect girls' weekend," I said, chewing my lip. "And I don't even know where to start."

"I can help," Jamie offered, perching on the chair opposite mine. She crossed one slender leg over the other and tugged at her pale green, scale-patterned leggings. One of the things I loved most about Jamie was her unique (and mostly marine-inspired) fashion sense. "Are any of the bridesmaids certified divers?" she asked, her expression thoughtful. "There's a great spot I could take y'all to about a mile past Coconut Cove."

I shrugged. "I'm not sure. I don't even know who the other members of the wedding party are just yet."

Jamie waved her hand. "That's okay. We could always go snorkeling instead. Or we could rent jet skis. There are lots of fun things to do out on the water." Her ocean-blue eyes widened. "Ooh! You could also take the girls dancing at the Lanai Lounge across town. Thursdays and Fridays are both ladies' night, so there's no cover."

"That's a great idea." I smiled at her, feeling a little better about my last-minute maid of honor duties. "I'll call Juls Kekoa after work and see if she can round up some last-minute luau tickets, too. By the way, you're welcome to join us—that is, if you don't have plans next weekend."

Jamie smirked. "Well, I *did* have a date with my couch and the final season of *Girls*, but I suppose I could clear my schedule."

"How generous of you," I teased. "What about that surfer guy you've been dating? No hot dates planned?"

Jamie's bottom lip poked out. "We had a major wipe out," she admitted. "I thought we were exclusive, but apparently, I'm not the only woman he's been seeing."

"Bummer."

She shrugged. "Meh. Plenty of other fish, right? The island's not *that* small." She waggled her eyebrows. "Who knows? Maybe I'll pick up a new man at the Lanai Lounge."

"Yeah, maybe." I smiled at her as I stood up and made my way toward the door. I poked my head out into the hallway. From the rear of the sales floor, I caught Happy Hula's assistant manager, Harmony Kane, giving me the stink eye. "Come on," I said, looking over my shoulder at Jamie. "Let's get back to work before the Wicked Witch of the East Pacific puts a hex on us."

The rest of the afternoon seemed to fly by, mostly because I was preoccupied planning Emma's bachelorette weekend in my head while I worked. By the time the boutique closed for the evening, I had come up with a list of activities that she was sure to love. I ran my ideas by Jamie as she gave me a ride home from work in her sea foam green Chevy Malibu, which I'd affectionately dubbed the Mer-mobile.

"Juls said she'd hold some tickets for us for the luau on Saturday night. Oh, and how does an afternoon at the resort spa sound?" I asked her, rolling down the passenger window so I could breathe in the ocean air as we sped past Coconut Cove. "I'm thinking mani-pedis, massages, maybe some time in the sauna. I could call Summer at the front desk tomorrow and book us for Saturday around noon. We can pack all the partying into Thursday and Friday and then recover with a little pampering before the luau."

"Sounds good to me." Jamie bobbed her head. "You know I'm always down for being pampered." She turned onto Kalapaki Drive, bringing the car to a stop in front of the teal and white beach cottage where I lived with my Aunt Rikki. There were two other vehicles parked in the driveway alongside my aunt's purple Vespa: a sedan driven by Rikki's ukulele teacher and a familiar black Jeep Wrangler. I cursed under my breath at the sight of the dark SUV, and Jamie gave me a curious sidelong glance. "I thought you'd be happy to see Noa."

"I am," I said, feeling sheepish. "I just didn't expect him to beat me here. I was hoping to grab a shower and freshen up before dinner, but I'd hate to keep him waiting."

Jamie grinned. "Just tell him you'll make it worth the wait."

I rolled my eyes. "Yeah, yeah," I said dryly. I stooped to snatch my purse off the floorboard. "Thanks for the ride. I swear one of these days I'm going to finally pawn off my old wedding band and use the money for a down payment on my own set of wheels."

"You've been saying that for weeks now. I'll believe it when I see it," she teased. "But in the meantime, I'm happy to give you a lift whenever you need it. See you at sunrise yoga tomorrow morning?"

"Only if you swing by and scoop me up so I don't have to run there with Rikki." My aunt insisted on jogging the two miles to the beach for our morning yoga sessions. I liked to think I was in fairly good shape, but I was *not* a morning person. Or a jogger, for that matter.

"You got it," Jamie chirped. She wiggled her fingers at me in a little wave before throwing the Malibu back into drive and speeding down the street.

I made my way up the gravel toward Noa's Jeep. The car still ticked with heat, so I figured it couldn't have been parked there for more than a few minutes. I paused in front of his side view mirror to check my reflection, wiping the smudged mascara from under my brown eyes. The dark brown roots of my hair were beginning to show above my golden highlights. I was either going to have to pop into a salon for a touch-up soon or commit to going back to my natural color. I frowned as my gaze fixed on the large, pink pimple currently taking up residence on my chin. If objects really were larger than they appeared, as the little label on the side view mirror claimed, then the bump could probably be seen from space. *Yuck.* I rifled through my purse in search of my concealer and quickly covered the blemish. *Better*, I thought, giving my reflection a satisfied smile. I tossed the makeup back in my bag and hurried toward the house.

When I entered the little beach cottage, I was greeted by the sounds of a gentle ukulele melody accompanied by a rich baritone voice. I followed the music toward the open double doors that led to our small backyard. My Aunt Rikki and her new ukulele instructor, Nani Johnson, were seated in white patio chairs on the lanai. Rikki clumsily strummed her instrument, doing her best to keep up with the tempo. Nani smiled and nodded at her encouragingly with each chord change.

Noa was perched opposite them on a wicker lounger. His eyes were closed, and a lazy smile spread over his face as he crooned the words to "I'll Fly Away."

Though I'd known him almost my entire life, I still got butterflies in my stomach whenever I saw Noa Kahele. We'd been best friends for as long as I could remember, though we'd drifted apart for the five years that I'd been married to Bryan. I had moved to Atlanta, while he had set off for Los Angeles to work for a tech startup. When I'd moved home to Aloha Lagoon at the end of June, I had been more than a little surprised to find Noa living on the island again. For the first time in our adult lives, we'd both been single. The only thing that had stood in the way of our romance had been our own insecurities. Of course, it hadn't taken long for our mutual attraction to overpower the doubt. We'd been casually seeing each other for a few weeks now, and I'd never been happier.

Aunt Rikki was the first to notice me standing in the doorway. She looked up from her ukulele, blowing a few loose strands of her black and electric-blue hair out of her face. Her fingers slipped off the fret, causing dissonance in her next chord. She didn't seem to mind.

"Good evening, *ku'uipo*," she called brightly, resting her uke in her lap. The word meant "sweetheart," and it had been her pet name for me since I was a small child. "How are things at the shop?"

"Everything's great," I told her, stepping onto the lanai to join the trio. "Hi, Nani." I nodded politely to the pretty brunette ukulele instructor and motioned for her to keep going when she paused midsong. "Don't stop on my account. You play so beautifully."

"Thanks." Nani beamed at me. "But we were just wrapping up, anyway. Rikki was showing off her skills to Noa. Your aunt's quite a fast learner."

I grinned. "Can't say I'm surprised." Ever since I'd come on board as the store manager at Happy Hula, Aunt Rikki had cut down her own work hours in order to pursue her passions. The music lessons were just the beginning of her new hobbies. Only twenty years my senior, my forty-seven-year-old aunt had boundless energy. In addition to learning the ukulele, painting, and making her own candles and soap, she'd also taken up salsa dancing. Rikki had briefly expressed an interest in beekeeping, and I was relieved when she'd changed her mind. Just the thought of thousands of the little bugs swarming in our backyard gave me hives.

Noa rose from the lounger and stretched his arms high above his head, giving me a nice view of his rippling biceps. "Hey, Kales," he said, using the nickname he'd called me since grade school. He came to stand next to me as Rikki and Nani put away their instruments. Noa's dark hair, which was nearly as long as mine, hung loose around his shoulders. He pushed it aside as he leaned down to plant a soft kiss on my lips, which sent a jolt of electric current down to my toes. There went those butterflies again.

"Keep practicing your C, F, and G7 chords," Nani instructed Rikki, gripping the handle of her instrument case as she rose from her chair. She said goodbye to Noa and me before my aunt walked her to the front door.

"I hope you're hungry," Noa said, slipping his arm around my waist and guiding me through the house after them. "I've got a craving for pineapple kabobs at Sir Spamalot's."

"Sounds good to me." I followed him toward the driveway, pausing on the front porch to give my aunt a quick peck on the cheek.

Noa held open the Jeep's passenger door for me before walking around to climb into the driver's seat. "Anything exciting happen at work today?" he asked when we were on the road a few minutes later.

"You could say that." I swiveled in my seat to face him. "My friend Emma called from Atlanta. Not only is she getting married the week after next, but she asked me to be her maid of honor. *And* she and the other bridesmaids are flying here next Thursday for her last-minute bachelorette party."

"Wow, that's great!" Noa took one hand off the wheel and placed it on my shoulder, giving it a gentle squeeze. "I guess that means I'll be flying solo next weekend."

"Actually, you'll be flying to Atlanta." I chewed my lip, suddenly feeling shy. "That is, if you'd want to be my date to the wedding. Emma asked for your information so that she could book our tickets on their return flight next Sunday morning. She and Dante insist on paying our airfare."

"Oh. Wow." Noa's forehead wrinkled. He released his grip on my shoulder and returned his hand to the wheel. I watched an uncomfortable look stretch across his face. "They don't have to do that."

I frowned. *Was it something I said?* "What's wrong?" I asked softly. "I mean. I know it's pretty last-minute. If you don't want to go—"

"It's not that," Noa said quickly, though he avoided my gaze. He pulled the Jeep into the small parking lot for Sir Spamalot's, an open-air eatery located directly on the beach. When he looked up at me, his troubled expression had vanished. "It's nothing," he said, smiling. "Really." He leaned over and kissed me on the cheek. "Come on. Let's get some grub—I'm starving." Without another word, he climbed out of the car and started toward the sand.

A knot formed in the pit of my stomach as I followed him. Things between us had been great for the past few weeks. We never fought, and Noa was always so attentive and kind. Still, though we'd been best pals for years, the whole romance thing was very new. Maybe asking him to be my date to a wedding on the other side of the country was crossing into Serious Relationship territory. *Does he think we're moving too fast?* Given his reaction to my invitation, I couldn't help but wonder.

Don't be ridiculous, I scolded myself. I removed my sandals and padded barefoot through the warm sand. *We've been on vacations before as friends. Just think of this as another fun trip together—maybe with some new, steamy perks.*

I shoved my worry aside and focused on the positives. I was on a dinner date in paradise with an amazing guy. In just over a week, one of my dearest pals was coming to visit, and she wanted me to help her celebrate the most important day of her life. I felt a rush of happy anticipation as I caught up to Noa, slipping my hand into his. I squeezed his fingers, and he pulled me closer, smiling down at me. Searching his eyes, I found no trace of the uncertainty I'd seen there before.

I grinned back at him. *See? Everything is going to be just fine.*

CHAPTER TWO

———

"What time was their flight supposed to land?" Jamie asked, craning her neck as she surveyed the crowd heading toward us from one of the terminals. It was the following Thursday, and we were seated at a bench in the Lihue Airport baggage claim area, waiting for Emma and her other bridesmaids to arrive.

I checked my watch. "About fifteen minutes ago," I replied. "They should be here any moment now."

With the help of Jamie and several crafting blogs on the internet, I'd spent the past week planning every last detail of Em's bachelorette weekend. Jamie had offered to take us on a guided snorkeling tour of Coconut Cove free of charge on Friday afternoon, and I'd called in a few favors with a few of the other Aloha Lagoon Resort staff to book some more fun activities. I'd even talked Aunt Rikki into donating some cute accessories for the gift bags we'd made for each of the girls. Jamie and I had also gone to the party supply store in Lihue before work on Wednesday to snag some tropical-themed decorations and favors. I couldn't wait to show Emma all of the goodies.

"What does she look like?" Jamie asked, squinting at a gaggle of college-aged girls who were crowding together to take a picture in front of a "Welcome to Hawaii" sign.

"Emma's about five-foot-four—and skinny, but not too skinny," I replied. "With hazel eyes and dark brown hair. The last time I saw her, she had a pixie cut."

"Got it." Jamie glanced at me, eyebrows raised in question. "What about the other girls?"

I shrugged. "No clue. I still don't know who else she asked to be in the bridal party." I chewed my lip, feeling the nerves bunch together in my stomach. I'd only met a handful of Emma's other friends, mostly sorority sisters from her college days at the University of Georgia. They'd seemed nice enough, but I'd never grown especially close with any of them. In fact, when I'd lived in Atlanta, I had been so consumed with managing a local dress shop and showing my support for my then-husband's football career that I hadn't made too many real friends. Emma was the exception. I'd met her at a spin class that one of the other football wives had dragged me to a couple of years ago. We'd bonded over trading snarky remarks about the instructor and his super tight bike shorts. After bumping into each other at a few more classes, we'd exchanged numbers and had become workout buddies and eventually great friends.

"*Kaley!*" I heard Emma's excited squeal before I saw her. She shimmied her way past a pair of middle-aged men in aloha shirts and broke through the crowd, practically skipping. Her hair was still cut in the same sleek, short style, and her smile was radiant as she bounded toward me. She emitted another shrill cry as she flung her arms around me and squeezed.

I hugged her back, feeling giddy myself. Though I'd made some incredible friends in Aloha Lagoon, seeing Emma relieved that tiny pang of homesickness I'd been feeling over the past couple of weeks. I didn't really miss Atlanta, per se, but I did miss hanging out with Em.

"I can't believe I'm finally here!" Emma gushed, squeezing me even harder. She released me and stepped back, beaming as she looked me up and down. "Girl, this Hawaiian lifestyle looks good on you—you're totally glowing."

"Thanks." I grinned back at her. "You look amazing, too. I love that outfit," I said, gesturing to her green and white, palm frond-patterned sundress and tan sandals with cork-wedge heels. "You're going to fit right in on the island." I turned and motioned to Jamie, who had risen from the bench to stand beside me. "Emma, this is my friend Jamie Parker."

Both Jamie and Emma were huggers, so it didn't surprise me when they embraced like old pals. My sandy-haired friend was quite a few inches taller than Em, so she had to stoop down to hug her, not that she seemed to mind. "Kaley's told me so much about you," she said cheerily.

"Likewise," Emma replied. "I hope you're planning to join us this weekend. We're going to have so much fun!"

"I wouldn't miss it." Jamie grinned. "We've got a few surprises planned."

Emma arched her eyebrow. "Do tell."

"Nope." I touched a finger to my lips and winked at her. "No spoilers. Now, come on! Show us the ring."

Emma's hazel eyes lit up. She lifted her left hand to show us the beautiful solitaire diamond that sparkled on her ring finger. "Isn't it gorgeous? It's a full carat."

"Wow," Jamie and I breathed in unison. I'd seen several pictures of the gem that she'd posted online, but they didn't do it justice.

"Are you showing off your engagement ring again, Em?" came an airy voice to my right. I glanced up to find a tall woman with mousy brown hair standing next to Emma on her other side. I studied the girl's slightly crooked nose and narrow face dusted with freckles, almost certain that I'd met her before.

As if reading my mind, Emma looked up, her gaze shifting from the newcomer to me. "Kaley, you remember Mia Miller, right? She was my roommate freshman year."

Oh, that's right. She'd joined us at the gym and for happy hour several times the previous summer. "Nice to see you again, Mia," I said to the tall woman.

Mia smiled. "You too," she said brightly. She gave Jamie a polite wave when I introduced her, and then she turned her attention back to Emma. "The girls should be right behind me," she said, glancing over her shoulder. "They stopped to take a few selfies in front of that beach mural outside our gate."

"I've been wondering who your other bridesmaids are all week," I said, raising a curious brow at Emma. "Who else is here?"

To my surprise, Emma avoided my gaze. "I think I see my suitcase," she said quickly, pointing at the baggage carousel. She took a few steps toward it.

Did she just deflect my question? My stomach clenched, and a feeling of foreboding crept over me. "Emma Jane Ross," I called, using her full name to get her attention. "What aren't you telling me?"

Emma stopped and turned around, her shoulders hunched. She and Mia exchanged a glance. Then she met my gaze and grimaced. "Kaley, just remember that I would never do anything to intentionally hurt you, okay?"

My own shoulders stiffened. "Okay," I said warily.

She chewed her lip. "Well, see, Dante asked Bryan to be in the wedding party—"

Oh no. "Please, tell me you didn't," I blurted, cutting her off. I had a sinking feeling I knew exactly who Emma had brought along.

Em's face pinched. "I had to," she said in a small voice. "He begged me to ask Val as a favor to Bryan. And then there's Coco, and she's family, so..." she trailed off. "It was hard to find anyone else who could be a bridesmaid on such short notice."

I opened my mouth to speak but closed it again as a nasal voice cut through the noise in the baggage area.

"Emma! Can you believe no one offered to take our carry-ons? I thought the people in Hawaii were supposed to be hospitable." A slender young woman with bleached blonde hair stalked toward us, her nose lifted high in the air.

I suddenly felt sick. The last time I'd seen Nicole "Coco" Becker, she'd been straddling my then-husband, shaking a pair of pompoms and wearing nothing but stilettos and a smile. She and two other Falcons cheerleader wannabes had been performing a *very* private routine in the bedroom I'd shared with Bryan for five years. Though we had been having trouble for a while leading up to the incident, it was the nail in the coffin for our marriage.

To add insult to my emotional injury, two of the three girls had actually gone on to make the squad. Coco—Emma's fiancé's Paris Hilton clone of a cousin—was one of them. The other was the tall, dark-haired bombshell walking beside Coco, with caramel skin and hips that would make even Shakira jealous. Her name was Valentina Cruz, and she was a former Puerto Rican swimsuit model—and, from what I'd heard, exotic dancer.

She was also my ex-hubby's new girlfriend.

Coco and Valentina glided to a stop in front of our little group. They were dressed in matching black track pants and red

Atlanta Falcons tank tops. The twin smirks that curled their lips at the sight of me set my blood to boiling.

"Hi, Kaley," Valentina said breezily, ignoring what I was sure was a stony expression etched on my face. "Long time, no see."

"Not long enough," I replied through clenched teeth, struggling to control my temper. *Wrecked any other marriages, lately?* I added silently.

Coco must have read my thoughts. She looked away, shifting her weight from one foot to the other as she nervously twirled a lock of her blonde hair around one finger.

Valentina, on the other hand, seemed to relish the fact that she'd turned my life upside down. She stepped forward, her dark eyes glittering. "Oh, come on." Even through her thick accent, I could hear the taunting slant to her words. "Can't we put our differences aside for Emma's sake? This weekend is about *her*, after all." Val's lips twitched. "Not you."

My nostrils flared. Though I was certain Valentina was trying to provoke me, she did have a point. I shot a glance at Emma, who was grasping Mia's forearm, her eyes darting nervously back and forth between the trampy pep squad and me. As much as I didn't want to, I was going to have to take the high road—for now, at least.

I stifled a sigh and forced my shoulders to relax. "You're right." I pasted a smile on my face, but it must not have been very convincing because I saw Mia cringe. I sucked in a breath and tried again. "Why don't I help you find your luggage?" I offered, looking from Valentina to Coco. I motioned for the two women to follow me to the conveyor belt full of baggage. Out of the corner of my eye, I saw Emma sag with relief.

I walked briskly toward the luggage carousel, thinking every foul word in the dictionary and even making up a few new ones. It had been Emma's choice to invite the two horrid women into her bridal party, and I had to respect that. Still, I was hurt that she hadn't warned me. Em knew what the terrible twosome had done to me, and having them show up here in Aloha Lagoon felt like a slap in the face.

Jamie caught up to me and leaned close. "*That's* your ex's new girlfriend?" she whispered. "What a witch."

I smirked. "That's one of the nicer words I'd use to describe her." We reached the conveyor belt and waited for the rest of the women to catch up. "I'm so glad you're here," I told her quietly. "I'm not sure how I'm going to make it through this weekend with my sanity intact." Until a few minutes ago, I'd been looking forward to the next few days. Now I was dreading them.

"I've got your back." Jamie squeezed my arm. "They're only here until Sunday, anyway. We can just drown ourselves in cocktails and ignore them." She gave me a toothy grin. "And it's not like things can get any worse, right?"

I wrinkled my nose. "Don't say that. You'll jinx me."

The others joined us at the baggage carousel. Coco and Valentina made their way toward the opposite end of the conveyor belt to retrieve their oversized bags as they came through the hatch. Emma grabbed her own suitcase and lugged it toward Jamie and me.

"Kaley, I'm *so* sorry," she said breathlessly. Remorse shone in her eyes. "I should have given you a heads-up about Coco and Val before we got here. I was afraid if I told you, then you wouldn't want to be a part of the wedding." Her head drooped. "I'm a crappy friend, aren't I?"

"I wouldn't go that far." I smiled. "Of course you're not a crappy friend," I said, patting her shoulder. "And it'll take more than those two to chase me off. I'm here for you, no matter what."

Emma tilted her head to peek up at me. "Good," she said, though her tone was still low and worried. "Because there's one other thing I should have mentioned before." Her gaze fixed on a point over my shoulder, and guilt flickered across her face. She inhaled sharply and then let her words tumble out in one breath. "Dante liked my Hawaiian getaway idea so much that he decided to do the same for his bachelor party. The guys are here too, and they're walking up right now. Please don't be mad!" She plastered a smile on her face as she dropped her bags next to my feet and waved at someone behind me. "Hey, baby!" she called. I barely had time to process what was happening before she took off through the crowd.

I turned on my heel to watch as Emma leaped into the arms of a broad-shouldered mountain of a man in a black Atlanta Falcons shirt and shorts. He was nearly six feet tall, with a chiseled jaw, black hair, and skin the color of creamy milk chocolate. Normally, I'd have been happy to see Em's fiancé, Dante Becker. He was a funny, charismatic guy, and we'd been good friends for several years. The problem was that he wasn't alone. As Dante untangled himself from Emma, I shifted my attention to the four men behind him—in particular, the blond, blue-eyed jerk standing slightly apart from the others. The air left my lungs, and I took a tiny step backward, feeling as if I'd just been sucker-punched.

"You have *got* to be freaking kidding me," I whispered, feeling heat surge through me. (Confession: *Freaking* wasn't the word I actually used.) "You really did jinx us," I told Jamie in a low voice, my gaze still fixed on my slimeball ex-husband, Bryan Colfax.

His dimples showed as he grinned back at me. If I were a less civilized woman, I'd have marched over and smacked the lazy smile off his stupid face. Hell—I was tempted to do it anyway, civility be damned. This was the man who had cheated on me with three women, resulting in a divorce that had been dragged through every news outlet from *ESPN* to *TMZ*. He'd caused me more humiliation than I'd ever thought I'd be able to bear. If there was anyone I loathed more than those two cheer skanks, Val and Coco, it was him.

Bryan made his way over to us, undeterred by my glare. "Hey, sweet cheeks," he said, his smile stretching even wider. "How've you been?"

Anger flared in my belly. He didn't have a right to call me pet names anymore. Our marriage had ended on terrible terms, and he was probably only being so chummy in case anyone happened to recognize him. Bryan had always cared more about his image than anything else.

"Never better," I said flatly, pulling away when he tried to lean in for a kiss on the cheek.

Bryan seemed to catch himself as I recoiled. He quickly straightened again, a fleeting look of embarrassment coloring his expression before his plastic smile slipped back into place.

"What were you thinking, coming back here?" I demanded in a low tone.

He shrugged. "You didn't think I'd miss a chance to return to Kauai, did you?" He swept his arm around in an arc. "Aloha Lagoon is like my second home."

I'd met and fallen in love with Bryan Colfax when he'd moved to Hawaii to attend college, but he'd been born and raised in a small Southern town. He'd dreamed of playing for the Atlanta Falcons since he was a kid, so when he'd been drafted, we had dropped everything and moved to Georgia. I should have realized it was a mistake to put my own life on hold to follow him clear across the country, but you know what they say about hindsight.

"Shouldn't you guys be at football practice?" I asked, gesturing to Dante and the other men. "The season kicks off in just a few weeks."

"Coach made an exception." Bryan's grin widened. "It's a special occasion, after all." His gaze roved over my low-cut purple tank dress and down to my bare legs, which were a shade or two darker and—thanks to Aunt Rikki dragging me along on daily jogs to sunrise yoga—a little more toned than the last time he'd laid eyes on them. "You look great, by the way."

I didn't respond. If Bryan thought he could charm me into forgiving him, he was going to be sorely disappointed.

"Of course she looks great," Jamie piped up from beside me. She brushed a few strands of sandy hair out of her eyes and stuck out her chin. "Kaley's practically glowing these days— breaking free from a toxic relationship has that effect on people." She tilted her face toward me, sending a wink my way but wincing as she caught sight of my face, which I'm pretty sure had turned an even darker shade of purple than my dress.

"Oh." Bryan knit his brows together, looking suddenly uncomfortable. He dropped his gaze to the floor as he collected himself. When he looked up again, he gave Jamie an amused smile. "Kaley, aren't you going to introduce me to your friend?"

I puffed out a breath. "Jamie, this is my asshat ex-husband, Bryan," I said flatly.

He ignored the barb and stuck out his hand. I felt a sense of satisfaction when my usually hug-happy pal didn't make a move to shake it. Bryan's cool facade began to crack, a hint of color forming along his collarbone and creeping up his neck. "Well, er, nice to meet you, I guess," he mumbled, letting his arm fall back to his side.

"There you are, babe." Valentina appeared at Bryan's arm, shooting me a dark look before wrapping her arms possessively around him and latching her lips onto his for a long, steamy kiss.

I met Jamie's gaze as I looked away. My expression must have shown my discomfort because she grabbed my arm with one hand and Emma's bag with the other, leading me away from the lip-locked couple. We moved close to Mia, who was lugging her suitcase off the conveyor belt.

Mia's eyes pinched in a look of sympathy. "Don't hold it against Emma," she said in her soft, airy voice. "Dante sprung it on her on Monday that he and the guys wanted to come to Hawaii too. She didn't have anything to do with it. And besides, they'll be off doing their own thing for the weekend. We probably won't even see them again until we head back to the airport on Sunday."

That was still too soon, in my opinion, but I kept that thought to myself. "Fine by me," I said, forcing a smile and trying not to sound as bitter as I felt.

Mia didn't fall for it. "I know it must be hard to see Bryan and Val like that," she said, giving me an understanding look. "If it's any consolation, they fight *all* the time."

As if on cue, an angry squawk erupted from Valentina. I turned in time to see her rear her hand back and slap Bryan across the cheek. She began scolding him in her native tongue, her words tumbling out in rapid succession. I couldn't understand what she was saying, but it didn't sound pleasant. Bryan's expression grew stormy. As we watched, he gripped his girlfriend by the wrist and pulled her away from the crowd, toward an empty corner near the restrooms. They continued to argue quietly.

Mia turned back to me and rolled her eyes. "See what I mean?"

My lips twitched. "I guess the honeymoon phase is over. I'm not letting them bother me, anyway," I told her. "I've moved on—I'm actually seeing someone here on the island." I felt my smile widen at the thought of Noa.

"That's great," Mia replied, beaming.

"So, does that mean I missed my window?" asked a rich, velvety voice. I looked up to find that Dante's other three groomsmen had walked over to the baggage carousel. One of them, a tall man with close-cropped sandy hair, was grinning at me.

I did a double take. "Will?" I stepped into his outstretched arms, laughing when he scooped me off my feet in a bear hug. "I almost didn't recognize you," I said as the man set me down. I stepped back so I could look him over. When I'd last seen Will Bolero the previous fall, he'd been a scrawny kid. The poor rookie kicker had been benched for months with a broken leg. Since then, he'd filled out and seemed to have bounced back from the injury. The muscles in his arms and chest rippled under his tight gray T-shirt. He looked more like he was ready to tackle someone than kick a few extra points.

"Wow. You're so...buff," I stammered. Out of the corner of my eye, I saw Mia bobbing her head in agreement.

"Physical therapy really helped," he said, giving me a modest smile. "And I've been on this high-protein diet for a while. It's worked wonders."

It certainly had. "You look fantastic!" I told him. "I'm glad your leg's all healed up."

"You and me both." He mimicked kicking a field goal and then pumped his fist in the air. "It's going to be a great season."

I introduced Jamie to Will and Dante's other two groomsmen, who also played for the Falcons. Freddy Jenkins, a short man with long dreadlocks, gave us a friendly hello. Tom Evans, a tall, bald man with a thick, muscular neck and permanent scowl, simply glared at me with silent disapproval. Tom had never been very warm toward me when I'd been married to Bryan, and I supposed our divorce hadn't improved his opinion of me. Oh well. It was no skin off of my back.

Once Emma had kissed Dante goodbye, we parted ways from the men, who were headed to the car rental agency. Jamie and I led the girls out to the passenger pickup area. Waiting at the curb was our own shuttle from Gabby's Island Adventures. I'd visited Gabby LeClair's office a few days earlier and explained my plans for Emma's special weekend, and we'd worked out an agreement where I could use the shuttle as a "party bus" for the evening. Jamie and I had decorated the inside of the vehicle with streamers and decals of pineapples, palm trees, and tropical flowers.

"Right this way, ladies," I said, gesturing for them to follow me onto the bus.

"Wow!" Emma breathed when she reached the top step. Her bright eyes went wide as she took in the decorations. "Kaley, this looks incredible."

"Thanks." I grinned at her. "Only the best for my favorite bride-to-be."

"Aloha," said the attractive young Hawaiian man sitting behind the steering wheel. He climbed out of his seat and stood to take Emma's hand. "I'm Koma, and I'll be your driver this evening."

Koma Pukui was an employee of Gabby's Island Adventures, and his chauffeur services came with the bus rental. With his dimpled smile, muscular frame, and bronze skin, he looked more like a model than a bus driver. His good looks weren't lost on the rest of the women, either. I glanced over my shoulder to find Mia eyeing him with her lips slightly parted. I was pretty sure I saw a little bit of drool.

"Where are all the dirty decorations?" Valentina griped when she stepped on board. She squinted as she surveyed the bus interior. "This looks more like a dinky luau-themed retirement party than a bachelorette bash." Nose crinkled, she ran a finger along one of the pineapple decals I'd placed on the window.

"Yeah—there's nothing naughty in sight," Coco agreed, copying Val's disdainful tone. Her gaze came to rest on Koma, and she licked her lips. "Actually, I take that back. At least you hired a hot stripper." She wedged past Mia and Emma and sat down in the first empty seat near the front of the bus. She licked her lips and crooked a finger at Koma. "Come to Mama," she said, patting her lap.

I shot Koma what I hoped was an apologetic look. "He's not a stripper," I told the lusty bridesmaid. "He's our driver."

Coco shrugged and continued to beckon for the young man to join her. "Well, you can drive me anywhere you want," she said, bouncing her eyebrows at him.

Koma's complexion turned a shade darker, and he dropped his gaze to the floor. "I should get back to my seat," he said, shifting uncomfortably.

Valentina settled in beside Coco. "What are these?" she asked, holding up one of the gift bags.

"Kaley and I put together some party favors," Jamie explained. She led Mia over to an empty seat and handed her one of the bags as the two cheerleaders tore into theirs. Jamie and I had filled the paper totes with colorful flowered leis, bracelets, and cute seashell earrings from the Happy Hula Dress Boutique, as well as T-shirts that I'd had custom made just for the bachelorette festivities. Each bridesmaid received a hot pink tank top with the words *Team Bride* screen-printed on the front.

"Still not even one penis," Coco muttered under her breath.

"Yeah, I didn't know this was going to be a PG party," Valentina said sourly. Neither woman sounded the least bit appreciative of the gifts. "No wonder Bry left her," she whispered to Coco, purposely loud enough for me to hear. "She's such a prude."

Don't let them get to you, I reminded myself. I did my best to ignore their whispered barbs and scooped Emma's goodie bag off the seat. "For the bride-to-be," I said, holding it up.

She took the tote from my outstretched hand and began riffling through its contents. "Kaley, this is amazing!" she gushed, holding up her own tank top, a white shirt with *Bride* printed on it and a pineapple in place of the letter *i*. She laid the top against her chest. "I can't wait to put it on." Emma placed the shirt back in her gift bag and then gave me a hug. "Don't listen to Coco and Val," she whispered in my ear. "I think all of this is perfect."

I beamed at her. As far as I was concerned, Emma's opinion was the only one that mattered. "I'm glad you like it."

We took our seats as Koma started the shuttle and drove us from the airport to the Aloha Lagoon Resort. The luxury destination was the epicenter of the little island town of Aloha

Lagoon, and most of the residents worked there in some capacity, me included. Koma rolled the little bus to a stop in the circular driveway in front of the resort's main lobby. Two bellhops hurried toward the bus and began to unload our luggage. One of them, a curly-haired man named Marco, avoided my gaze when I stepped off of the bus. We'd crossed paths a few weeks before when I'd been trying to get my Aunt Rikki out of a jam, and, well…let's just say he wasn't my biggest fan.

"This place is gorgeous," Mia said, climbing off of the shuttle right behind me. "Like, totally pic-worthy. No filter needed." She pulled her phone out of her purse and walked over to the side of the building, snapping photos of the beautiful man-made lagoon.

"No kidding," Emma said, giving my arm a squeeze. Her gaze roved over the cream-colored building with its tiled terra-cotta roof. "The pictures on the website don't do it justice." She grinned. "I can't believe you live here."

"Well, I don't live *here*," I corrected her. "I'm staying with Aunt Rikki at her place, just a few miles away."

She rolled her eyes. "You know what I mean, Kaley. You live in paradise." She sighed. "This is so much cooler than Atlanta."

I just smiled. She was right about that.

Jamie excused herself to go back to her own apartment to get ready for our first night out. While she headed to her car in the employee parking lot, I led the rest of the group through the sliding double doors and across the granite floor of the lobby. After checking in with Summer behind the front desk, we turned down the hallway that led to the ground-floor suites. Emma had booked two adjacent rooms that were connected through a door on the inside. I handed the envelope of key cards for the first room to Mia, who was staying with Coco and Valentina. Emma and I would be staying together in the other bedroom.

Marco wheeled a luggage cart into the first room while the other young bellhop wrestled Emma's overstuffed suitcase toward our doorway. "You can just leave it right here," Emma said, motioning to the space beside the entrance. "I can take it inside." The bellboy did as she asked and accepted a few small bills from Em with a grateful nod before retreating down the hallway.

"After you," I said, grinning as I motioned for Emma to enter the room first.

She returned my smile. "Thanks." Practically buzzing with excitement, Emma gripped the handle of her luggage and dragged it into the room. She'd only made it about ten steps before she skidded to a halt. Her grip on the suitcase loosened, and it toppled sideways onto the floor as she let out a piercing shriek.

CHAPTER THREE

———

"Oh my gosh!" Emma gasped. She paced around the room, taking in the huge, glittering banner that read *Congratulations, Future Mrs. Becker!* on the wall above one of the two queen-sized beds. On the bedside table sat a vase with a gorgeous bouquet of hibiscus, plumeria, and other tropical flowers. Pink and white streamers hung from the ceiling above the couch, and a silver tray of macadamia nuts, chocolate covered strawberries, and pineapple chunks was arranged on the coffee table, along with a bucket of ice with a bottle of champagne chilling inside. I'd enlisted the housekeeping staff to put up the decorations for me while Jamie and I'd gone to the airport to pick up Emma and the other girls. I'd also given them a little white envelope with Em's name on it. It was leaning against the ice bucket, and Emma stooped to pick it up. She tore open the paper and gasped with pleasure at the Aloha Lagoon Resort spa gift card she found inside.

"That's your gift from me," I told her, grinning. "We're all getting mani-pedis on Saturday afternoon, and I've already booked a massage for you as well." Though Dante had offered to pay for everything else, I'd scraped together enough extra money to spring for Emma's spa treatment myself.

Emma set the card back on the table and turned to face me, her hazel eyes brimming with tears. "Kaley, you didn't have to do all this. Thank you."

"You're welcome." I walked over to the table and popped open the bottle of champagne, filling one of the flutes. "You should check out the view." I gestured to the double doors that led to the room's private veranda. I handed Emma the glass of champagne and then poured one for myself before following her outside. I breathed the warm, salty air blowing in from the ocean, which was visible from the little patio. "Happy bachelorette weekend," I said, holding up my glass to toast her.

Emma gently clinked her champagne flute against mine. "You're the best," she said. She cast her gaze out toward the ocean, and her eyes became clouded. She remained that way for several long moments, as if lost in thought.

"Is everything okay?" I asked gently.

"Yeah," Emma said absently, her attention still fixed on the waves. "Just prewedding jitters. You know how it is." She brought the glass of champagne to her lips but stopped, her eyes widening a fraction. "Oh! I almost forgot." She set her drink down on the bamboo patio table. "I got you something," she said, scurrying back inside.

I raised my eyebrows, surprised. "Em, you shouldn't have," I said as I followed her into the bungalow, sipping my champagne as I went. I relished the sensation of little bubbles fizzing on my tongue. *Mmm.*

Emma had dragged her oversized luggage to the foot of her bed and was crouched beside it on the floor, rummaging through its contents. She tossed a few dresses over her shoulder and onto the bed. "Ah!" she cried, removing something from the bottom of the pile. "Found it." She swiveled to face me and held up a large box wrapped in pink paper and gold ribbon.

Curious, I took the present from her outstretched hands and gave it a subtle shake. Something large but not too heavy shifted inside.

"Go ahead and open it now." Emma picked herself off the floor and grabbed the dresses she'd thrown aside, carrying them over to the closet. She hung them up and then perched on the corner of her bed, smiling at me expectantly. "Come on. I can't wait to see the look on your face."

"All right." I gently tore at the wrapping paper, trying not to look as apprehensive as I felt. I'd never been entirely comfortable opening presents in front of people. There was always so much pressure to *ooh* and *ahh* just the right amount so that the person knew you liked their gift—even if you didn't and were just being polite. It was something I'd hadn't quite mastered, considering I was a terrible liar.

Luckily for me, I didn't have to feign the cry of excitement that escaped my lips as I removed the rest of the wrapping and opened the box. Nestled inside the crumpled tissue paper was a beautiful, black Michael Kors satchel purse. In fact, it was the exact handbag that I'd shown Emma several months before when we'd been window shopping at Lenox Mall one Sunday afternoon in Atlanta. I'd debated whether or not I should buy it, but despite her encouragement, I'd ultimately decided against it. Bryan and I had just filed for divorce, and I'd known my funds were going to be limited in the very near future.

"Wow, Em," I breathed, running a hand over the black leather. "You *really* shouldn't have. This is too much."

"Oh, hush," she said, beaming. "I bought all my bridesmaids new purses as a thank you for helping me get ready for my big day." She rose from the bed and came to stand beside me, peering into the box. "Besides, I know how much you wanted that bag, and it is *so* you."

I lifted the purse out of the tissue and slid the cross-body strap over my shoulder, admiring my reflection in the mirror on the wall. "You're right about that." I grinned.

Emma nodded. "Of course I am. Now come on. Let's get ready so we can meet up with the others for dinner."

Em had requested that all of the girls wear little black dresses for our first night out, so I opened my own suitcase and quickly shimmied into a form-fitting tube top dress I'd purchased with my employee discount from the boutique the week before. After curling my long brown hair and refreshing my makeup, I helped Emma squeeze into her own outfit. As the woman of the hour, she'd chosen to wear a lacy white Ralph Lauren cocktail dress and gold pumps. She'd used a straightener to make her short, dark hair flip out at the ends, and her makeup was flawless.

"How do I look?" Emma asked, twirling in a slow circle. "I was going for bombshell bachelorette." She winked.

I felt my eyes mist. "Well, you nailed it," I said, clearing my throat when my voice came out hoarse.

"Are you crying?"

"No," I fibbed, but I was pretty sure the sniffle that followed gave me away. "I'm just so happy for you—and you look absolutely stunning."

Emma smirked. "If you think *this* dress is hot, just wait until you see the one I have for the wedding," she said, her eyes twinkling. "It kills."

"I'll bet it's gorgeous," I replied with a nod. "I can't wait to see it."

A knock sounded at the door, and Jamie's voice filtered through from outside. "I'm back," she called. "Is everyone ready?"

I quickly transferred my wallet, phone, and a few other essentials into my new purse. "One more thing," I said to Emma as we stood outside the other bungalow. "You have to put these on." I handed her a pink sash with the words *Bride-to-Be* scrawled across it in glittery gold lettering, along with a gold tiara.

"Thanks!" She slipped the sash over one shoulder, and then I helped her clip the tiara into her hair. We opened the door to meet Jamie just as Mia, Coco, and Valentina spilled out into the hallway from the room next door.

Val and Coco wore almost identical black slip dresses. Coco had accessorized hers with a long gold chain and sparkly, black wedge sandals, while Valentina had opted for pops of color with her bright red shoes and matching lipstick. Mia wore a silky, sleeveless tunic that I was almost certain we carried in stock at Happy Hula.

After fawning over Emma's appearance for a few moments, our group turned and headed toward the main lobby.

"Did you get settled in okay?" Jamie asked Mia, pausing to adjust the ankle strap on one of her black pumps.

Mia and I stopped beside her while the others continued down the hall. "I don't know if *settled* is an appropriate word," she replied, cutting a look at her weekend roommates. "Bunking with those two is like living on the set of a reality TV show." She rolled her eyes and picked a piece of lint off her dress.

The Real Homewreckers of Atlanta? I suppressed a smirk. "That bad, huh?"

Mia grimaced. "Coco and Val are BFFs in public, but behind closed doors, it's a nonstop catfight. Coco's jealous that Bryan picked Valentina over her after the whole…well, you know." She briefly met my gaze before looking away again.

"It's okay," I told her. "You can say it. The affair."

"Right." She lifted her eyes to mine. "Val's been rubbing it in her face. On top of dealing with *that*, she's been trashing you every chance she gets, and Coco hasn't exactly been singing your praises, either." She chewed her lip. "Sorry, Kaley. They really don't like you."

I shrugged. "I can't say that I'm surprised." The animosity was mutual, anyway. I could barely stand the sight of the cheer tramps.

We caught up to the rest of the group as they reached the elevators, and we went up a few floors to Starlight on the Lagoon, one of the island's finest restaurants. With Dante's credit card information and his blessing, I'd reserved a table at the upscale eatery to kick off Emma's bachelorette festivities. After a delicious dinner and a round of drinks, we headed back downstairs and piled into the party shuttle, which was waiting for us in the circular driveway in front of the main building. When we were all on board, Koma pulled the bus away from the resort and headed out on the town.

I'd reserved a VIP booth at the Lanai Lounge, Aloha Lagoon's premier nightclub. The hot spot was located across town from the resort. Though it was a short distance, Koma was kind enough to drive the shuttle around a few extra blocks so that we could make the most of our time on board. He weaved in and out of traffic and rolled down the winding roads along the shoreline, letting us take in the view of the sun setting over the ocean.

"All right, *wahines,*" Koma called from the front of the shuttle after about twenty minutes. "Are you ladies ready to party?"

There was a chorus of cheers from the girls as he parked in front of the Lanai Lounge. The nightclub was housed in a building designed to look like a giant totem pole. The carvings on the exterior glowed pink and green, and a neon green sign with the nightclub's name was fixed just above the entrance. A line had formed in front of the building, and loud dance music could be heard through the open door. I thanked Koma as we climbed off the bus, and he promised he'd be back to pick us up as soon as we were ready.

"Just give me a buzz," he said, holding up his cell phone.

As Koma pulled away in the shuttle, I led the group straight up to the bouncer, a man named Javier Morales. I'd met Javi at the resort, where he sometimes offered personal-training sessions to the guests on weekdays at the gym. He was also a good friend of Noa's. At six feet tall, Javi was a brick wall of muscle. He stood with his arms crossed over his barrel chest, the neon light of the nightclub's sign glinting off his shiny, bald pate.

"Hey, Jav," I said brightly as I strolled to the front of the line.

The brawny man looked up, and his face broke out into a grin. "Kaley! How's it going, girl?" He glanced past me and then met my gaze, eyebrow lifted in question. "Where's your man?"

I smirked. "At home. It's ladies' night." I gestured to the rest of the crew. "We're celebrating. I've got one of the VIP booths reserved."

Javier gave an approving nod and stepped aside to let us through the door, much to the dismay of the line of women waiting to get into the club. "You girls have fun tonight," he shouted over the chorus of protests.

The inside of the Lanai Lounge was designed to look like a large outdoor veranda. The ceiling was painted with a mural that featured a colorful sunset on one side of the room and faded into a dark sky on the other. LED lights winked on and off like twinkling stars. Fake palm trees lined the walls, and the tables and chairs set up around the club resembled cushy patio furniture. The VIP booths were nestled in private cabanas along the far wall.

"Let's grab a drink before we get settled," I yelled over the loud music as I gestured to the bar. We each perched on one of the wicker stools, and I reluctantly took the empty space next to Valentina. Her shoulders were hunched as she tapped vigorously on her cell phone screen. Judging by the frown tightening her glossy lips, I assumed she was engaged in a text argument with Bryan. *Not my problem*, I thought, though I might have felt a tiny bit of smug pleasure that my ex and his rebound fling were fighting yet again.

Emma leaned over the bar, saying something into the ear of a tall, blond bartender with a surfboard tattoo on his left shoulder. The young man grinned and nodded before stooping to grab several shot glasses from under the counter. Em turned around to face the group. "I'd like to kick off the party tonight by buying all my favorite girls a shot."

The bartender set down five small glasses in front of us and then handed a larger one to Emma. "A double of our best tequila for the bride-to-be," he said, bowing slightly. "It's on the house. Congratulations."

Emma beamed at him. She took the glass and then turned to us, lifting it high in the air. "To all of you awesome ladies—and especially Kaley, for organizing what I know is gonna be an incredible vacation." Her smile widened as she clinked her glass against mine. "Here's to a weekend we'll never forget!"

* * *

The Friday morning sunlight filtering through the window woke me with unforgiving brightness. I tried to open my eyes but immediately squeezed them shut again, feeling a wave of pain roll through my head. *Holy hangover.*

I gingerly lifted my head and squinted across the room at Emma. She was lying in the opposite direction as me, with her toes resting on a pillow and her head dangling off the foot of the bed. A lock of short brown hair hung limply over her eyes, and her complexion was edging into undead territory. She looked as bad as I felt, possibly worse. "Need the trash can?" she croaked, gesturing weakly to the little plastic waste bin on the floor beside her bed.

"Maybe." I eased myself into a seated position, shutting my eyes as my mind replayed blurry memories of the previous night. Images of the crowded dance floor flashed through my head, making me dizzy all over again. I sank back down onto the bed and waited for the feeling to pass.

After several more minutes, Emma and I slowly began our morning routines. While she showered, I paced around the large bedroom, overturning every accent pillow and piece of discarded clothing in search of my new purse. It was nowhere to be found. "Just great," I muttered, irritated. The bathroom door opened, and I glanced up to see Emma standing in the threshold, her body and wet hair wrapped in matching white towels. "I can't find my purse," I told her.

Emma's dark eyes seemed to look straight through me. Though freshly showered, she still looked ill. Her lips were pressed tightly together, and her forehead bunched. After a moment, she shook her head, as if snapping out of a trance, but her troubled expression remained. "Huh?" she asked, blinking at me.

"My purse," I repeated, trying not to sound as grouchy as I felt. "I must have left it on the bus—or maybe at the club." My heart sank into my unsettled stomach. *My brand-new bag.* The generous gift that Emma had given me twelve short hours ago was gone.

She grimaced. "I'm so sorry. We could try calling the club. Maybe someone turned it in."

"Yeah, maybe," I said, though I wasn't hopeful. Some jerk had probably found it and had helped himself to the contents of my wallet. The purse would likely wind up on eBay. Another frustrated groan poured out of me. "My keys and my phone were in there, too." I was going to have to get a new cell and warn Aunt Rikki to change the locks on the house *and* the shop. This was turning into one expensive mistake.

I used Emma's phone to call my own. It rang several times before my voice mail recording played. Next I went online to check my bank statement and credit card accounts. After seeing that there was no new activity, I was feeling a little more hopeful. Perhaps I'd just left my purse on the party bus rather than in the nightclub. Our driver, Koma, was a preacher's son, and he seemed trustworthy. If he'd found my belongings, they'd be safely stowed at the office of Gabby's Island Adventures until I went by to claim them. I called and left the owner, Gabby LeClair, a message to see if my bag had been turned in and then gave Emma her phone back before taking my own quick shower.

Until I heard back from Gabby or Koma, I'd try not to stress too much. This weekend was about celebrating Emma, and I couldn't let my drunken blunder ruin the fun.

Emma and I met up with the others at the resort's breakfast buffet. Jamie had been scheduled to work a half shift as the morning cashier at Happy Hula, but she dropped by to grab a quick bite with us on her way into work.

"Good morning," she said brightly as she took a seat next to me at our table. She spread a pat of melted butter on a warm coconut muffin and then took a bite. "Mmm," she moaned, closing her eyes. "This is perfection." She waved over a server carrying a drink tray. "I'd love a coffee, please." She glanced around the table at the rest of us. "What about you ladies? Anyone ready for their first mimosa of the day?"

"No," Coco groaned loudly.

"No thanks." Emma held up a hand to wave off Jamie's offer. "I'll stick with water. We've got a long weekend ahead of us, so I should probably pace myself and rehydrate."

"Same here," Mia agreed.

Jamie gave me a knowing look as I also declined the cocktail. "Suit yourselves," she chirped in her impossibly cheery tone. I loved her to death, but her ability to recover from a wild night of partying in ten seconds flat was just plain unfair.

"Could you not talk so loud?" Coco groused. She rubbed her eyes, smearing what was left of last night's mascara. "My head is killing me."

"I guess Valentina decided to sleep through breakfast," Emma said, looking around the table.

Mia glanced to the empty seat next to hers and then shrugged one shoulder. "I haven't seen her this morning. She was already up and out of the room when we woke up."

"Maybe she got up early and hit the gym," Coco said.

Emma grimaced. "How can she work out first thing this morning after all the drinks she had last night?"

"I went for a three-mile jog and took a sunrise yoga class this morning," Jamie said, still sounding annoyingly perky.

Coco shot her a dark look. "Maybe Val went to Bryan's room," she mumbled.

I glanced over at her, but she quickly dropped her gaze down to her coffee mug, lifting it from the table and taking a sip. I shrugged. I'd be lying if I said I wasn't glad to have a break from Valentina myself.

I hadn't planned any special activities for the morning, having assumed that the girls would want a few hours to recover from our wild night before we joined Jamie for some snorkeling later that afternoon. Just as I'd suspected, everyone agreed that we should take it easy until lunchtime.

Once we'd finished our breakfast, Jamie went to work her shift at the boutique while the rest of us changed into our swimsuits for a morning of relaxing by the pool. Valentina still hadn't returned to the room she was sharing with Mia and Coco, so they left a note to let her know where she could find us.

Though I'd known he wasn't working the early shift, I couldn't help but feel a little disappointed when we arrived at the swimming pool and Noa wasn't sitting in the lifeguard chair. In his place was Remy Hendricks, a blond, bronze-skinned Brit who closely resembled a young Daniel Craig.

"Mmm," Coco murmured as she settled onto the lounger closest to his post. She lowered her sunglasses and stared at Remy. "Maybe I should pretend to drown so he'll give me mouth-to-mouth."

I fought back a smirk. "I don't think you're his type." I laid my beach towel across one of the loungers and waved at Remy, who returned the gesture with a broad grin.

"What? And you think *you* are?" Coco challenged. "What do you have that I don't?"

Humility? Class? A personality? Take your pick. I'd been about to explain that Remy preferred men, but her attitude rubbed me the wrong way. "You know what?" I said, forcing a chipper tone. "You're right. Maybe you two would hit it off. Why don't you go talk to him?"

Coco lifted her chin. "I think I will," she said snootily. She smoothed her bleached blonde hair and adjusted the straps of her green bikini top. Then she riffled around in her bag, pulling out a compact mirror and a tube of lipstick labeled *Mother Pucker.* After applying a fresh coat of the gloss, she dropped the makeup back into her purse and rose to her feet. Untying the sarong from around her waist, she dropped it onto the lounger and strutted toward the hunky lifeguard, seductively swaying her hips. I flinched when I caught an eyeful of her ample backside through her thong.

Mia followed my gaze and made a face. "Yikes. That is *way* more of Coco than I ever needed to see."

"No kidding," I agreed. I turned away from the blonde cheerleader and gestured to Mia's beach bag. "Can I use some of your sunscreen?"

"Sure." She retrieved a little blue bottle of SPF-50 lotion and handed it to me.

I glanced over at Emma, who was reclining on the lounger beside Mia's, playing with her phone. "Any chance you might have missed a call about my purse?" I asked hopefully as I slathered the lotion onto my shoulders.

"Let me check my call log." Em tapped at the screen for a few seconds and then shook her head, giving me a sympathetic smile. "Nothing yet. Sorry, girl. I'm sure it'll turn up soon." Her expression turned thoughtful. "Wait a sec. I've got an idea that might help us track it down."

"I'm all ears," I said, tossing the lotion bottle back to Mia.

Emma met my gaze. "Remember when someone stole my phone at the gym last year, and we found it with that GPS tracking app?"

I felt my whole face light up. "That's right! I'd completely forgotten." Emma had managed to recover her missing cell before it had even made it out of the building. I'd been so impressed that I had downloaded the app for my own phone on that same day. We'd linked our accounts so that we could track each other's devices in case it ever happened again.

Em handed me her phone. "As long as your battery isn't dead, we should be able to track it to within about fifty feet of its location."

I pulled up the locater app, pumping my fist with excitement when the little pin appeared on the screen. "It's working!" I squinted at the little map, feeling a rush of cool relief. "It says my phone is right here at the resort. Koma must have found it on the bus after all and taken it back to Gabby's office." I zoomed in on the map and felt my relief turn to confusion. "Wait. That can't be right," I muttered.

"What's wrong?" Mia sat up and leaned forward so she could see the screen, too. "Where is it?"

I turned the phone around so that she and Emma could see the little dot, which appeared to be close to the boardwalk that led to the beach near Ramada Pier. "It looks like it's on the beach," I said, unable to contain my surprise. "But how did it wind up out there?"

"Maybe your purse really was stolen," Mia replied, frowning. "Whoever took it must be near the shore."

I rose from the lounger and gathered my things. "I'm going to go find it."

Emma's forehead wrinkled. "What if the person who took it is dangerous?" she asked, her tone laced with trepidation. "Maybe I should go find Dante and make him come with us."

"There's no time," I told her. "Whoever took my purse might be gone by the time Dante gets down here."

"I'll go with you," Mia offered. She turned and gave Emma an encouraging look. "Come on, Em. We'll be fine if we stick together."

Emma was still for a few moments, her face twisted as if she were struggling to make up her mind about something. Finally, she nodded. "Okay," she said. She turned toward Coco, who was still standing next to the lifeguard chair. "Coco, we're headed to the beach," she called.

The short blonde waved us off. "Have fun," she yelled back, never taking her eyes off Remy. I stifled a laugh when I saw her reach over and trace a finger along one of his biceps. Remy took a small step back, shifting his weight uncomfortably. Coco seemed oblivious to his disinterest, and she continued to flirt with the lifeguard as Mia, Emma, and I left the pool patio.

We made our way to the boardwalk that led to the stretch of beach reserved for resort guests only. The shore hadn't yet been warmed through by the sun when I slipped off my shoes, and an involuntary shudder worked its way down my spine as the cool sand touched my skin. The beach was surprisingly empty for midmorning, with only three of the resort-owned lounge chairs occupied by guests. A young couple was jogging along the shoreline several hundred yards from the pier. The rest of the area was deserted.

"Think one of these people has your phone?" Mia asked, scanning the other beach-goers.

I checked the map. "No. According to this, it's past the lounge chairs," I said, pointing.

Emma frowned. "But there's no one over there."

I shrugged and started in the direction that the map indicated. Emma and Mia followed, and a few minutes later we were standing in a quiet part of the beach. I surveyed the sand, but there was no sign of my purse or the phone. "I don't understand," I said, puzzled. "It's supposedly within fifty feet of where we're standing."

"Why don't you try calling it?" Emma suggested. "Your phone isn't dead, or we wouldn't be able to track it, right? Maybe we'll be able to hear it ringing."

Figuring I had nothing to lose, I dialed my number and waited. A few seconds later, my ears perked up as the chorus to Bruno Mars' "Uptown Funk" sounded faintly somewhere to our right.

"That's your ringtone, isn't it?" Emma asked.

I nodded but held up a finger to my lips, signaling for her to stay silent so that I could focus on the sounds coming from my missing phone. The call went to voice mail, and I hung up and immediately redialed. I began walking toward the sound, straining to hear. My excitement mounted as the music grew louder. I was glad I'd turned the phone's volume all the way up at the club the night before, otherwise I'd probably never have heard it over the sound of the waves slapping against the shore. I was so focused on listening for the ring tone that I wasn't paying attention to where I was walking. My foot caught on something in the sand, and I gave a startled cry as I lost my balance and tumbled to the ground.

"Kaley! Are you okay?" Emma sprinted toward me with Mia on her heels.

"I'm fine." I sat up, dusting the sand off my legs. I pressed redial once more and waited for my phone to start ringing again. To my surprise, it sounded as if I were right on top of it.

Mia crouched beside me. "*X* marks the spot," she joked. "Where's one of those kids with a plastic bucket and shovel when you need 'em?"

I didn't respond. I shoved my hands into the sand and started working to unearth the object that had tripped me. My hands closed around soft leather. I could feel my phone vibrating as I gripped the object and lifted it. "My purse!" I cried, elated. I tugged at the bag, but the strap was stuck to something under the sand.

Mia frowned. "What is it wrapped around?" she asked.

"A piece of driftwood, maybe," I said, gritting my teeth as I pulled harder. Mia began to dig in the sand below the bag, trying to loosen it.

A moment later, we both screamed. I let go of the purse and skittered backward, sending a spray of sand through the air. My purse strap wasn't stuck on a piece of driftwood.

It was wrapped around the corpse of Valentina Cruz.

CHAPTER FOUR

———

"Ms. Kalua, I wish I could say it's a pleasure to see you."
The portly Polynesian man standing in front of me nodded,
giving me a smile that didn't quite reach his eyes. His name was
Ray Kahoalani, and he was a homicide detective for the Aloha
Lagoon Police Department.

I understood his sentiment, and the feeling was mutual.
While Detective Ray was a kind, courteous man, our paths only
crossed when something bad had happened—like finding my ex-
husband's lover in a shallow, sandy grave, for instance.

The detective glanced over his shoulder at his team, who
had already set to the task of blocking off the patch of beach
where we'd found Valentina. We'd immediately stopped digging
after our grisly discovery, and I'd used Emma's phone to call the
police. Now a petite Asian woman from the coroner's office who
had introduced herself as Dr. Aimi Yoshida was crouched low in
the sand as she studied the corpse.

Valentina's body was slumped in an unnatural position,
and several clumps of darker sand were scattered around her
head, matching the rust-colored streaks on her left temple. The
shoulder strap of my new purse was still wrapped across her
body, and my stomach lurched at the sight of dried blood that
coated the leather in several places. I wouldn't be getting the bag
back anytime soon—though, after seeing it on a corpse, I wasn't
so sure I wanted it.

Shuddering, I turned away from the dead woman,
pulling my bathing suit cover-up more tightly around me. I
couldn't bring myself to look too closely, but from what I had
seen from a quick glance, I had the sinister impression that she
hadn't died by natural causes. *So much blood*, I thought, going

queasy all over again. As much as I'd disliked the woman when she was alive, I wouldn't have wished her such a gruesome death.

I looked at Emma, who was huddled next to Mia on one of the nearby loungers, sobbing. Her beach towel was wrapped around her shoulders like one of those emergency blankets that EMTs often gave to accident victims. Mia sat close to Emma, staring at the sand. Though she was no longer crying, her shocked expression suggested she was equally traumatized.

"Did you hear me, Kaley?" Detective Ray's voice punctured my thoughts.

I blinked rapidly and then shifted my gaze back to him. "I'm sorry," I said, feeling heat creep into my cheeks. "What was the question?"

"I asked when you last saw Miss Cruz alive," the burly detective repeated. Though his tone was patient, his lips drew down ever so slightly at the corners.

I sucked in a mouthful of sea air and then forced it slowly back out. "She was with us when we returned to the resort," I said, squinting as I concentrated on my hazy, alcohol-soaked memory. "We'd all been out drinking and dancing at the Lanai Lounge for Emma's bachelorette celebration. When we arrived back to the hotel at a little after midnight, Emma and I headed straight to our room." I frowned in concentration as I reached back through my cloudy recollection. "I think I remember hearing Val say she wanted to keep the party going. She was planning to drop by The Lava Pot for another drink."

"Did she go alone?" The detective's bushy eyebrows lifted in question.

A light clicked on in the back of my mind. "Now that you mention it, I don't think so." I frowned. *Coco.* In all the chaos of the past half hour, I'd completely forgotten about her. My gaze shifted from the detective to Emma and Mia. Had either of them called the flighty blonde to let her know that her cheer mate and friend had been killed? Or was she still at the pool, oblivious to the tragedy as she flirted with Remy the lifeguard?

"Can you elaborate?" Ray commanded my attention again. "Who accompanied Miss Cruz to The Lava Pot?"

My eyes snapped back to him. Despite his patient expression, I detected a slight look of irritation in the creases around his eyes. "I think Coco might have—Nicole Becker. She's one of the other bridesmaids." I gestured to Emma and Mia. "We left her by the pool when we came out here to track my phone. I haven't seen her since."

"Your phone," Detective Ray said, flipping to a new page in the little notepad that he carried in the pocket of his loud-patterned aloha shirts. His gaze locked with mine, and I felt a sense of unease. Though at first blush, the man's demeanor seemed laid-back and kind, I was picking up a subtle suspicion beneath his easygoing exterior, and it rattled me.

"Kaley, how do you suppose your purse and phone wound up buried in the sand with Miss Cruz?" he asked.

My mouth went dry. "I have no idea," I said honestly, though my voice cracked on the last syllable. I'd seen the detective in action before, and the trace of mistrust in his tone didn't bode well for me. I did *not* want to end up on the wrong end of his investigation.

Detective Ray's eyes narrowed a fraction at the hitch in my voice. Lips pressed together in a straight line, he wrote something else down on his notepad and then looked up at me. "You said you went straight to your room when you returned to the resort around midnight. Did you leave again at any point?"

"Not until this morning." I shook my head. "We had breakfast about an hour and a half ago."

"Can anyone corroborate your whereabouts for the rest of the evening?"

I blinked. He wanted someone to vouch that I had stayed in the room all night. *Does he think I'm lying?* "Of course," I said, hiking my thumb in the direction of the lounger where the other girls were still seated. "Emma and I are sharing a room. We were both there all night."

I felt a hint of relief when Detective Ray shifted his gaze away from me, but it quickly vanished. He motioned for me to follow as he started toward Emma, making it clear that he wasn't done with me just yet. He introduced himself to the two women and then raised his notepad. "Can you state your full name for me please, miss?" he asked Emma.

She dabbed at her soggy eyes with her towel. "Emma Jane Ross," she replied, her voice hoarse.

"How did you know Valentina Cruz?"

Em flinched and dropped her gaze to the sand. "This was supposed to be a fun weekend vacation," she said quietly. "I'm getting married in a few days. Val is—she *was*—one of my bridesmaids. And now she's..." Her voice died away. Emma's complexion lightened several shades, and she clutched at her stomach. "I don't feel so good," she moaned, rocking back and forth on the edge of the lounger.

Mia wrapped a protective arm around Emma's shoulders. "I think she's in shock," she said. "She just needs a few minutes to calm down. I could walk her down the beach for a bit while she composes herself," she offered. Mia met my gaze. "Or maybe you'd want to go with her, Kaley."

I shook my head. "No. You go ahead—if it's okay with the detective, I mean." I glanced at Detective Ray. "Is that all right?"

He studied the two women for a moment, probably trying to decide if either posed a flight risk. Finally he nodded. "Just one more question first," he added, holding up a finger. "Miss Ross, you were sharing a room with Ms. Kalua. Once you arrived back at the resort from the night club, did you both remain in the room for the rest of the evening?"

Emma shook her head. "No," she replied softly.

It was my turn to be confused. "No?" I blurted, gaping at her.

Emma flashed me a guilty look. "I went to Dante's room after you fell asleep." She shifted her gaze to Detective Ray. "Dante Becker is my fiancé," she explained. "He and his groomsmen are also staying at the resort for his bachelor party." She flicked a glance at me and then dropped her eyes, looking embarrassed. "We haven't spent more than a few nights apart since we started dating, and I have trouble sleeping when he's not in the bed with me. I went upstairs to his room and stayed there until just before sunrise." Emma looked up again, meeting the detective's gaze. "He can confirm that if you talk to him."

I stared at my friend, suddenly feeling sick to my stomach. I'd had no idea that I'd been alone in our room after falling asleep. Emma's confession that she'd left for several hours put a serious dent in my alibi. Would Detective Ray think I'd lied to him on purpose?

The burly man flicked a glance in my direction. As if reading my mind, he asked Emma, "Was Ms. Kalua in the room when you left to visit your fiancé?"

Emma frowned. "I think so," she said, avoiding my gaze. "I left the lights off so I wouldn't wake her when I sneaked out." She clutched her middle again, and a soft groan escaped her lips. "I'm going to be sick." She doubled over and began to hyperventilate.

Mia stooped beside Emma and rubbed her back. She shot Detective Ray a pleading look. "Can you give her just a minute?" she asked, her tone filled with concern.

"Don't wander too far," he told her. "I have some more questions for you both."

Mia quickly helped Emma to her feet and ushered the sick girl several yards down the beach. I took a few steps after them but halted when Detective Ray cleared his throat. I turned around to find him watching me. "Can anyone else confirm that you stayed in your room for the rest of the night?"

I gulped. "No."

The detective nodded. He fixed me with another probing look. "Did you know Valentina Cruz before she arrived on the island?"

Crap. I had no choice but to tell him the truth. I swallowed, dreading the inevitable turn his questioning was about to take. "I met Val when I lived in Atlanta," I said, fighting to keep a neutral tone. "She's dating my ex-husband, Bryan."

Detective Ray raised an eyebrow. "Interesting."

I felt beads of perspiration forming under my arms. I could practically see the gears turning in the man's head, deducing that jealousy or revenge could have been my motive. He was quiet for several moments while he looked at me as if waiting for me to continue.

The silence was unnerving. "Maybe you should talk to him," I blurted, feeling my palms begin to sweat. "He's also staying at the resort."

Ray's other brow lifted to join its twin. "Your ex-husband—Miss Cruz's boyfriend—is here on the island?"

The guilt came in a sudden rush. I'd just thrown Bryan under the bus to divert suspicion from myself, and it was too late to backpedal. "He's one of Dante Becker's groomsmen," I hedged. "They arrived yesterday afternoon."

"What is Bryan's last name?"

"Colfax." I tried to ignore the sour feeling in the pit of my belly while silently praying that he wouldn't ask me any more questions.

Luck was on my side. Detective Ray turned away from me to flag down one of the uniformed officers as he passed. I noticed with a pang of sadness that the other man was carrying the clear, plastic evidence bag that contained my blood-soaked purse. After murmuring something to the officer that I couldn't hear, Ray dismissed the man and returned his attention to me.

"I'll pay Mr. Colfax a visit once I've finished speaking to your friends," he said. "But first, I'd like a list of the names of everyone in the wedding party."

"Sure," I said, trying to keep my voice even. I told him the names of the other groomsmen. When he'd dismissed me, I watched him head across the sand toward Emma. My friend was on her knees in the surf. Mia crouched beside her, holding back wisps of dark hair from Emma's face while she gagged. I grimaced and looked away. *Poor Em.* On top of the hellish hangover and wedding planning stress, she'd just experienced a terrible trauma. Though I wanted to help, there was nothing I could do for her right then. She and Mia still had to give their statements to Detective Ray, and in that moment I wanted to get as far away as possible from the beach, the police, and Valentina's body. I made my way over to the wooden boardwalk that led back toward the resort courtyard.

"Kaley!" A familiar voice carried my name across the sand. I raised my head and scanned the edge of the beach. A small crowd had gathered on the boardwalk, with onlookers craning their necks to see what was happening beyond the police blockade. Cool relief flooded through me as I spotted Noa near the front of the cluster of guests. I quickly closed the gap between us, ducking under the yellow police tape.

"I got here early for my lifeguard shift," he said, folding his arms protectively around me. "I found out about the body as soon as I stepped into the lobby. Summer said the girl who died checked in with your bachelorette crew last night. I tried calling you a few times, and I got worried when you didn't answer. So, I called Rikki and then came looking for you." Noa squeezed me. "I'm so sorry, Kales. Are you all right?" he asked softly.

I sagged against his chest, moisture pricking my eyes. "No," I said, my voice ragged. Hot tears slid down my cheeks, and he held me while I cried. "Can we get out of here?" I asked after a few moments. Several curious pairs of eyes had turned our way, peering at me with interest.

Noa nodded in understanding. "You got it."

I stepped out of his embrace and took his hand. Together, we pushed our way through the sea of people and hurried down the boardwalk. We didn't stop until we reached the courtyard next to the merchant area of the resort. I perched on the edge of a bench several yards from the entrance to one of the Olympic-sized swimming pools, and Noa dropped down beside me.

"Do you want to talk about it?" he asked softly. His expression became strained. "It wasn't your friend, was it? Emma?"

"No," I said quickly, and his face instantly relaxed. "Emma's okay, but she's very upset."

"Understandable," Noa replied, pulling me closer. "What happened?"

I wiped the last few tears from my eyes and then swiveled so that I was facing him. I filled him in on my missing purse and how we'd tracked my phone to the beach. He listened quietly, his brow furrowing deeper with worry as I explained that we'd discovered my bag buried in the sand with Valentina's body. "And apparently Emma sneaked out of the room to be with Dante after I fell asleep last night, so I don't have a solid alibi." I sighed. "You should have seen the way Detective Ray looked at me when he found out Val was my ex-husband's new girlfriend. If I hadn't panicked and told him that Bryan was here too, he'd probably be hauling me down to the station right about now."

Noa stiffened. "Bryan's here?"

Uh-oh. My stomach sank down to the courtyard tiles. I hadn't seen Noa since before I'd gone to the airport to pick up the girls, so I hadn't had a chance to tell him about my ex's unexpected arrival along with the rest of the wedding party. He and Noa had never gotten along, largely because Noa had harbored feelings for me since we were in high school. When I'd left the islands to marry Bryan, it had driven a wedge between Noa and me for years. We'd only recently reconciled. Just the mention of Bryan in conversation was enough to make Noa brood—having him back on the island might tear open those old wounds.

"I didn't know he was coming," I explained, feeling guilty. "But I should have told you as soon as I ran into him."

Noa looked at me through hooded eyes. "You've talked to him?" Though he tried to hide it, I detected the hurt in his voice. Noa was the most confident, charming man I'd ever met. Could he really be so insecure about me speaking to my cheating, scumbag ex? He had to know there wasn't a snowball's chance in a volcano that I'd ever consider taking Bryan back. *Right?*

I sucked in a breath and pushed it out slowly. "Yes," I said. "I spoke to Bry at the airport—very briefly. He just wanted to say hello, but I gave him the cold shoulder." I frowned. "Emma was worried I'd cause a stink if she'd told me ahead of time that he was going to be here. She also failed to mention that she'd asked two of his cheer sluts to be in the wedding party." I was struck by a sudden flash of anger, but I forced it down. My feelings about my ex and his mistresses weren't important right now. One of the women was dead, and someone on the island had killed her.

And I just pointed the police straight toward Bryan. Detective Ray was going to find my ex-hubby as soon as he'd finished taking statements from Emma and Mia. Though I knew that news of the death had already spread around the resort, the victim's identity may not have made it all the way through the resort gossip mill just yet. What if Bryan was innocent? *Then he might not even know that Val is dead.* The horrible realization struck me like a bolt of lightning. It was possible that he was about to be blindsided when the detective showed up to question him about her murder. *And it'll be my fault.*

"I've got to find him," I said suddenly, rising from the bench.

Noa blinked at me. "Huh? Find Bryan? But you just said—"

"I know." I held up a hand as I cut him off. "But put yourself in his shoes. What if something happened to me?" I shuddered inwardly at the thought. "How would you feel if you didn't find out until the cops were knocking down your door to accuse you of hurting me—or worse?"

His expression became pinched. "I'd be devastated," he admitted.

"Then you understand why I need to get to Bryan before Detective Ray does. If he doesn't know that Val is dead..." I trailed off, feeling another rush of guilt.

Noa squinted at me. "Are you sure you're up to that, though?" he asked softly. "I mean, haven't you already been through enough trauma this morning?"

Though he was trying to be supportive, I thought I detected a hint of vulnerability in his voice. Was he really jealous of my ex?

"Yes, I'm sure," I said, giving Noa a pointed look. "It's the right thing to do."

"Of course." He stood up and placed his hand on the small of my back. "I'll go with you—for support," he added quickly when I blinked at him in surprise. As badly as I disliked Bryan, Noa hated him tenfold. I wasn't sure it was a good idea to put the two of them in the same room together, but I didn't protest. Truthfully, I was glad to have him by my side.

"Fine," I said, giving him what I hoped was a grateful smile.

Noa pulled out his phone as he followed me toward the resort's main building. "I'm going to call Remy and ask if he can stay longer and cover my lifeguard shift," he said. "Once we've found Bryan, I'll take you home so you can get some rest. You must be exhausted."

"I'm all right," I insisted, gesturing for him to put the phone away. Adrenaline could work wonders as a hangover cure—I was as alert as if I'd had a shot or two of espresso with a Big Gulp of coffee for a chaser. "Besides, Emma was a mess when I left the beach. I should stick close by in case she needs me when she's done giving her statement to the cops."

"That's so kind of you," Noa said, beaming at me as he dropped his phone back into the pocket of his board shorts. "Emma is lucky to have you for a friend."

"She'd do the same for me," I told him. "Em and I have always had each other's backs." *At least, she used to have mine,* I added silently. Maybe I didn't deserve Noa's praise. Though I did want to be there to support my friend, I also wanted to talk to her about her late-night disappearing act. Could Emma really not go a single night without being with Dante? If that were the case, why would she have initially booked the trip to Hawaii without him? I couldn't shake the feeling that there was something that Em hadn't wanted to tell Detective Ray.

Or maybe something she hadn't wanted to say in front of me, I thought, recalling the way she'd refused to meet my gaze. Had it been guilt from knowing that, by telling the police her whereabouts, she would ruin my alibi? Or was there something else she was hiding?

CHAPTER FIVE

———

When Noa and I reached the main lobby, we made a beeline for the concierge's desk. Summer was working that morning, and though she smiled when she saw us, her eyes were pinched with sympathy. "I'm so sorry about your friend, Kaley," she said as we reached the counter.

The term *friend* wasn't one I'd use to describe Valentina Cruz, but I had nothing to gain by speaking ill of the dead. "Thank you." I gave her a half smile and leaned across the counter. "I need to find her boyfriend," I said, my tone low and urgent. "He's staying here at the resort with four other men. I don't think he knows what's happened yet, and I need to tell him before he learns about it from the press." *Or the police.*

"Sure." Summer's gaze shifted to her computer monitor, and her hands moved over the keyboard. "What's his name?"

I glanced around the crowded lobby. A woman in a wide-brimmed beach hat was browsing a rack of excursion brochures and pamphlets at the far end of the front desk. She seemed preoccupied with an unfolded *Nature Lovers* map of the island, probably looking for one of the many hiking trails near the cliffs that overlooked the ocean. Aside from her, no other guests were within earshot. I exhaled with relief.

Lowering my voice so that it was just barely above a whisper, I asked, "Do you have any rooms booked under the names Dante Becker or Bryan Colfax?"

Summer's pencil-thin brows rose. "Bryan Colfax? Isn't that the name of your ex-hus—" She seemed to catch herself. Summer looked from me to Noa and then tucked her chin. "Sorry," she said, her tone sheepish. "I didn't mean to pry."

"It's okay," I said evenly. I wasn't surprised that she knew what had happened between Bryan and me. The details of my divorce had made national headlines thanks to my ex's star athlete status, and gossip on the resort spread faster than wildfire. I thought for a minute, trying to recall one of the aliases that the guys sometimes used to book hotels when they wanted to travel incognito. "If you don't see rooms under either of those names, try Dasher Byrd. It's the moniker Bryan gives when he doesn't want nosy reporters or paparazzi finding out where he's staying."

Noa snorted. "A running back for the Falcons uses the alias Dasher 'Bird'? Isn't that a little on the nose?"

Summer smirked in agreement as she tapped away on her keyboard. A moment later, her smile vanished, and she blinked at the screen. "How about that? There *is* a Dasher Byrd staying in one of the luxury suites on the top floor."

I gave myself a mental high five. "Great! Can you give us the room number?"

It wasn't until Summer was writing the information down for us on a piece of resort stationary that I noticed the woman who had been browsing the brochure rack had moved closer. She was hovering just behind Noa. Though her face was still hidden behind the map, I detected a nervous energy in her posture. As Summer slid the sheet of paper toward me from across the counter, the mystery woman peeked around the side of the map, and I caught a glimpse of her face. Recognition shocked through me, accompanied by white hot anger.

Felicity freaking Chase.

Felicity Chase was a journalist for the local paper, the *Aloha Sun.* She was also an insatiable gossip. She'd take any tidbit thrown her way and run with it, crafting the most salacious stories for the *Sun's* entertainment column and social media posts. In fact, after stalking some of the resort's celebrity guests, she'd been banned from stepping foot on the property—which, I supposed, was why she was skulking around with her face hidden behind the tourist map. She must have heard about the murder and camped out in the lobby, waiting to catch someone she could pump for details.

"You shouldn't be here, Felicity," I growled at her.

Realizing she'd blown her cover, the reporter dropped the map on the counter. Noa whirled to face her, and in one swift motion, she sidestepped past him and snatched the piece of stationary from the counter. "Thanks for the lead!" she sang as she sprinted toward the elevators, her chestnut tresses flowing behind her.

Summer reached for her desk phone. "I'll alert security," she called as Noa and I darted after the woman.

Noa had almost caught up to Felicity when a group of children wandered through the lobby and right into his path. He halted abruptly, and I almost collided with his back as I skittered to a stop behind him. A harried-looking young mother ushered the kids along, oblivious that her little clan had hampered our pursuit. The diversion gave Felicity the few extra seconds she needed to reach an open elevator and slip inside. She grinned at us, wiggling her fingers in a taunting little wave as the double doors closed.

I swore under my breath. "We can't let her get to Bryan," I said breathlessly.

"Room 732, right?" Noa asked, meeting my gaze. "That's what Summer wrote on the paper?" I'd barely nodded a confirmation before he turned and raced toward the door that led to the stairwell.

I removed my flip-flops and ran after him, taking the stairs two at a time. My morning jogs with Aunt Rikki hadn't quite prepared me for dashing up six flights of stairs. By the time we reached the seventh floor, my heart was pounding in my ears, and my chest felt as if it were going to explode. Noa pushed open the door at the top of the stairwell, and we tumbled into the hallway. Felicity's elevator must have been held up on a floor or two, because she was still standing outside Bryan's room, her arm raised and hand poised to knock.

"Stop!" I yelled, running toward her with a burst of renewed energy.

"Sorry," she called back, offering me a smug expression. "I need a big story for this week's paper, and this is too juicy to pass up. The murder of a star athlete's lover?" Her mouth curved in a wicked grin. "Sorry, Kaley. It's nothing personal." Felicity turned around and rapped her knuckles on the door.

In a fit of rage, I did the only thing I could think to do. I threw both of my flip-flops at her. The first spongy shoe hit her cheek with a soft *smack,* and the second pelted against her leg.

Felicity whirled to face me, surprise and anger flashing in her eyes. "Did you just—"

Her words were cut short as I plowed into her, shoving her out of the way. "Bryan!" I cried, banging on the door. "It's Kaley. We need to talk."

Noa reached us just as Felicity recovered from my attack and lunged at me. She tried to wedge her way in front of me, but Noa gripped her arms and pulled her backward. "Get your paws off me!" she snarled.

As the three of us grappled in the hallway, the door to the suite opened. One of Dante's other groomsmen, Tom Evans, loomed in the threshold, his broad shoulders blocking our view into the room. "What do you want?" he asked, his dark, angry eyes boring a hole into my forehead.

I took a step back, bumping into Noa. He released his grip on Felicity, which gave her a chance to dart in front of us.

"Hi, there! My name is Felicity Chase, and I'm a reporter for the *Aloha Sun.* I'd love to get a comment from you about the terrible tragedy that occurred this morning." She tried to peek around the big man. "I understand the murder victim was the girlfriend of Falcons' running back, Bryan Colfax. He's staying in this room, correct?"

Felicity shrank back when Tom shot her a withering look. "We don't talk to reporters," the bald man growled in his deep, Vin Diesel–like bass.

"But I just—" Felicity began, but he cut her off.

"Go," he warned.

"Is Bryan in there?" I asked, stepping around the flustered journalist. "I didn't know if he'd heard about Valentina yet, and I—"

"He knows," Tom said. His jaw clenched. "And you're the last person he wants to talk to right now. You're poison."

"Hey, watch it, brah." Noa was at my side in the blink of an eye, his chest puffed out and the vein in his neck straining with barely controlled anger. "You can't talk to her like that."

Tom eyed him, as if noticing him for the first time. A look of amusement flickered across his features before the scowl slipped back into place. "Son, you do *not* want a piece of me."

I gulped. Though Noa was in great physical shape, he was no match for the massive pro linebacker. He might get in a few good licks, but if Tom wanted to, he could pound him into the carpet without breaking a sweat.

"Noa," I said, my tone soft but urgent. "It's okay." I met Tom's gaze. "We'll leave." The man had never liked me, and everyone's emotions were high right now—which was understandable, given the circumstances. I'd come to deliver the news to Bryan, but it was too late. He already knew. At least he'd found out before the police showed up. Plus he had his friends to console him. The best thing we could do at the moment was go. *But first...*

"There's just one thing," I added in a tiny voice, feeling my guilt resurface. "The police may show up wanting to ask Bryan a few questions."

A vein throbbed in Tom's forehead. "What did you do?" he growled.

I held my hands out in front of me in a placating manner. "Nothing. I just—"

"Leave Bryan alone," he said, glaring at me. The warning in his tone was unmistakable. "He's been through enough this year without you causing even more trouble." Tom stepped back, giving me a momentary glimpse into the room. Dante, Freddy, and Will were gathered around Bryan, who was seated on a chair in the far corner with his head in his hands. I felt my face go slack as I caught sight of Coco Becker kneeling beside him, speaking in a low tone while she gently rubbed his back. *What is she doing up here?*

Before I could say anything, Tom slammed the door in my face. Hard. I sighed. "He's never been my biggest fan," I muttered to Noa.

"Why not?" The question came from Felicity. For a moment, I'd forgotten she was still there. I turned to find her standing behind Noa, her gaze ping-ponging back and forth from me to the closed door. She flashed me that familiar, predatory smile she wore when she thought she'd found a juicy story hook.

"That man's a football star too, right? Do you also have a romantic history with him?" Her face lit up, and I could see the whites of her eyes. "Let me guess—he asked you out, but you rejected him, and he's still a little bit hurt about it. *Or*"—her smile grew even wider—"were you still married when Mr. Tall, Dark, and Stormy made a pass at you? That would make a much better angle."

I glared at her. *I've got an angle for you*, I thought, seething. My hands balled into fists at my sides. The elevator dinged at the end of the hall, and I quickly uncurled my fingers. Fighting with the shady reporter wasn't worth my time. "You're one hell of a 'reporter,' Felicity," I said, pouring as much sarcasm as I could into my tone. I turned to Noa. "Come on. Let's get out of here." I no longer cared if the she stuck around—with Big Tom Evans serving as the bouncer for Bryan's suite, there was no way she was going to pester anyone in that room.

I turned to find the resort's head of security, Jimmy Toki, stepping off the open elevator. "Miss Chase," he boomed as he stalked toward us.

The smile disappeared from Felicity's face, and I felt a sense of satisfaction when she gulped audibly. The journalist was quick to recover. "Yes, I know," she said with an exaggerated eye roll. "I'm not allowed on the premises. I need to get back to the office anyway," she added, giving me a snide grin. "I've got a story to write." She started down the hallway. "I'll see myself out."

Jimmy stepped in front of her, his bulky frame blocking her path. "I don't think so," he said gruffly. "I don't want you lurking around the resort and harassing our paying guests—*or* our staff," he added, looking at me over her shoulder. I smiled gratefully back at him, but he didn't break from his intimidating character. Though I knew Jimmy personally and considered him to be one of the friendliest guys on the island, I'd seen him in action before in his security role. I would hate to be on his bad side.

"Whatever." Felicity stuck out her chin. She darted one last look over her shoulder at Noa and me before Jimmy ushered her into the elevator. I sagged with relief when the doors closed behind them.

Noa glanced at his watch. "I need to head down to the locker room to change into my swim trunks before my lifeguard shift." He looked up at me, his brow creased with concern. "Are you sure you don't want me to take you home?"

I forced a smile. "If I didn't know any better, Mr. Kahele, I'd think you were trying to weasel out of working today."

He grinned, showing off the kind of dimples that most Hollywood A-listers had to sell their souls to their plastic surgeons to achieve. "Maybe I am. If it means I get to spend more time with you, then it's worth a smaller paycheck." Noa's gaze moved from me to the closed door of Bryan's suite. His expression turned serious. "Do you think he could've killed his own girlfriend? Don't they always look at the spouse or boyfriend first?"

I sighed and retrieved my flip-flops. "I don't know, but I think this time, I'm going to leave it up to Detective Ray and his men to figure it out." The last time I'd been involved in an investigation, I'd wound up in danger. I would much rather leave the crime-solving to the professionals. It was their job, after all. Plus, I had other things to worry about, like consoling Emma and doing my best to ensure she got the bachelorette weekend she deserved, despite the tragic circumstances.

Noa and I took the elevator this time, crowding in with five surprisingly fit elderly women in bikini tops and sarongs. We wedged our way into one of the back corners and rode in silence as the ladies chattered excitedly about their morning hula dancing lesson.

"You're going to need a new phone," Noa said as we stepped off on the ground floor. "Even if it's only a temporary replacement."

"Oh, right." I sighed. In all the excitement, I'd forgotten that my phone was sitting in a plastic evidence bag—along with my keys and wallet. In addition to needing to obtain a phone, at some point, I was also going to have to run back home to Rikki's to retrieve my spare key, passport, and emergency credit card.

"Why don't you get up a little early tomorrow morning and I can take you to pick out a new phone before your plans with Emma and the other girls?" Noa offered. He grimaced. "Assuming they'll be up for any more festivities after all this."

I squeezed his arm. "That's sweet of you to offer. I'll let you know once I've checked on Em—I'll pop by the pool before your shift ends." I gave him a quick kiss. "Thank you for being so supportive. I know having to be on the same flight back to Atlanta with Bryan on Sunday isn't exactly your idea of a good time. If I'd known he was going to be here, I would have warned you."

Noa's face clouded. "The flight on Sunday," he repeated, his tone troubled. "I don't think that's such a good idea."

"What?" I felt my face go slack. Was he really bailing on me right now?

Noa crossed his arms over his chest. "How is it going to look to the police if you hop on a cross-country flight after your ex-husband's girlfriend has just been murdered—with your purse found on her body?"

"Oh." I shut my mouth with a click. He had a good point.

"And besides," Noa continued, frowning. "The police might not even let anyone from the wedding party go home until they find out what happened to Valentina."

I took a step back, feeling my chest tighten. I hadn't thought of that either. *Emma wouldn't be able to make it back in time for her own wedding.*

Noa must have read my emotions in my expression. "Hey, I didn't mean to upset you," he said softly. "I'm sorry." He took my face in his hands and tilted my chin so that I was looking up at him. "I need to get to work, but I'll see you later." He gave me a soft peck on the lips before turning to go.

I watched as Noa headed down the hall that led to the employee locker room, feeling suddenly sick to my stomach. I hoped he was wrong about the police holding the wedding party here until they caught Val's killer—but that wasn't the only thing about his words that was bothering me. *Does he still seem like he really doesn't want to go to the wedding?* Perhaps I hadn't been imagining his hesitation before. Did Noa secretly think that being my wedding date meant we were getting too serious too soon? Was he having second thoughts about whatever was happening between us?

Stop it, I scolded myself. Now wasn't the time to fret about my love life. I shoved the doubts aside and turned to head in the opposite direction of Noa, stepping through the double doors that led out into the courtyard. Before I went back to the room to see how Emma was doing, I needed to make a quick stop in the Happy Hula Dress Boutique. I hadn't checked in with Aunt Rikki since the news broke about the murder among the wedding party, and she was probably worried sick about me.

It was early afternoon, and the lunch rush of shoppers had died down, leaving the store mostly empty with the exception of a handful of guests and the employees on duty. Rikki was in my face before I'd even made it halfway to the front counter.

"Are you okay, *ku'uipo*?" she demanded, the collection of bangle bracelets on her wrists jingling loudly as she threw her arms around me.

"I'm fine," I wheezed. As usual, she was squeezing me so tightly that she was nearly cutting off my oxygen.

My aunt released me and stepped back. She was dressed in a white linen tunic over floral leggings, and her black hair with its electric-blue streaks was pulled up in a bun that was held together with a pair of bright yellow chopsticks. Rikki's dark brows narrowed. "Why didn't you tell me Bryan was in town? You should have called me," she scolded.

It was the first time in years that she'd used a reproachful tone with me. My Zen, flower child, *Aloha-is-my-way-of-life* aunt didn't dislike many people, but she *hated* my ex-husband.

"I would have warned you," I said quickly. "But I lost my phone last night, and, well—it's sort of a long story." One that I didn't want to tell in front of the few nosy shoppers who were watching us as they pretended to browse the nearby clothing racks.

Rikki harrumphed. "That man brings bad energy with him everywhere he goes," she said, frowning.

"Kind of like you, Kaley." A tall, slender woman in a black dress and hot pink espadrilles smirked as she strode toward us. "After all, wherever you go, dead bodies turn up."

An elderly woman perusing the beach towel display cut a look in our direction, and I could practically see her ears perk up.

"Can it, Harmony," I said through clenched teeth. Growing up, Harmony Kane had been the island's resident mean girl and my high school rival. Now, through a cruel twist of fate (or, rather, my aunt's noble yet unwarranted penchant for giving people second, third, and twentieth chances—everyone except Bryan, anyway), we were coworkers. Though Harmony and I had recently formed an unlikely alliance during a dangerous situation, we weren't exactly BFFs. Frenemies might be a more appropriate term—and even *that* was too strong a word for the most part.

Harmony shrugged. "What?" she asked, her tone indignant. "It's true."

I ignored her. "I just dropped by to let you know that I'm all right since I couldn't call," I told Rikki. "Now that I'm temporarily without a working cell phone." I avoided a curious look from Harmony. "But I need to go check on Emma now. She should be finished speaking to Detective Ray by now, and when I last saw her, she was in pretty bad shape."

Rikki frowned. "The detective sent one of his men in here, too, *ku'uipo*. He asked to speak with Jamie. They're in my office right now."

My chest tightened. Why would the police want to talk to Jamie? *Relax*, I told myself silently. *Either Mia or Emma must have mentioned that she went out with us last night. Of course the police would get her statement, too. You have nothing to worry about.* Despite my best efforts, the inner pep talk did nothing to ease the lump of dread taking root in my middle section. It was my gut's way of telling me that perhaps I should make myself scarce before the officer emerged from Rikki's office.

I gently grabbed my aunt's arm and pulled her away from Harmony. "Tell Jamie to come find me when she gets off work. I'll be in the room I'm sharing with Emma for the weekend."

Rikki nodded. "Of course." She squeezed my hand. "If your poor friend needs anything, come to me. I have a few teas at home that can cure anything from grief to stress or even the most stubborn Charley horse."

I couldn't help but grin. Only Aunt Rikki would think that grief could be soothed with a hot cup of tea. "I love you," I said, giving her a quick peck on the cheek before I ducked out of the shop and back into the bright July afternoon. I retraced my steps into the main building and walked down the hall in the direction of the rooms Emma had booked for the weekend. I'd only made it halfway down the hall when I heard someone call out my name from behind. I turned to find Jamie sprinting toward me.

"Rikki said I just missed you," she said breathlessly.

"I didn't want to be there when the police came out," I admitted. I met her gaze. "They found my purse—it was buried in the sand with Valentina's body."

Jamie paled. "That explains a few things," she said, her worry clear in her voice. "The officer asked a lot of questions about you."

My heart rate sped up to a gallop. I swallowed. "What kind of questions?" I asked, though I had a sinking feeling I already knew the answer.

Jamie grimaced. "He wanted to know how you were acting around Valentina last night. He asked if you'd threatened her or said anything to me about her that could be interpreted as a threat. Then he asked if there was anything strange about your behavior at breakfast this morning."

I felt my heart drop down to my toes. Questions like that could only mean one thing.

The police were seriously considering me as a suspect in Valentina's murder.

CHAPTER SIX

———

"So, I take it we're probably not still on for snorkeling this afternoon?" Jamie asked, attempting a smile, though I could still see the worry behind her eyes.

"I doubt it," I said wearily. "I was on my way back to the room to check on Emma. I'll see if she and the other girls are feeling up to it, but I wouldn't hold my breath. I think this morning put us all through the ringer."

Jamie squeezed my arm. "Is there anything I can do for you or the others?" she offered.

I shrugged. "I honestly don't know," I told her. "I think we all just need to take the afternoon to decompress."

She nodded in understanding. "In that case, I'm going to head to my apartment and take a cat nap. I'll meet back up with you here at the resort in a few hours." She gave me a hug. "I know you didn't do it, Kaley. If you need help proving that to the police, just say the word and you know I'll have your back."

"Thanks," I said, returning her hug. I watched Jamie retreat down the hallway before turning and trudging in the opposite direction. I felt hopeless. Detective Ray had let me go earlier, yet the questions he and his men were asking about me could only mean that they'd placed me on their short list of possible suspects. Maybe he'd done some digging into my past conflict with Valentina and had discovered the news coverage of Bryan's cheating scandal. Or was it possible that someone else had pointed him toward some of those old articles during their own statement, hoping to cast suspicion on me and draw attention away from himself or herself? If so, who?

I found myself wondering if perhaps Bryan really could be guilty. I hadn't meant to implicate him in my conversation with the detective, but I couldn't rule out the possibility that he could have murdered his own girlfriend. After all, Noa had been right—the significant other was most often the culprit. If their passionate-reunion-turned-equally-passionate-quarrel at the airport the day before was any indication, Bryan's relationship with Valentina was far from perfect. I recalled Val sitting at the bar of the Lanai Lounge the night before, tapping angrily at her phone. Had she been fighting with him again? Maybe they'd met up on the beach after we'd returned to the hotel so they could continue their argument in person. I assumed Bryan had probably been pretty hammered himself, having been out celebrating Dante's last few days as a bachelor. If the couple had a drunken argument, could it have escalated to the point of violence? I'd seen Bryan angry before many times during our marriage, but he'd never come close to physically harming me. No, from my experience, emotional and psychological barbs were his weapons of choice.

Then again, that was just the version of Bryan that I had known—the one who'd sometimes verbally abused me but had always remained faithful. *Until I found out he hadn't been faithful after all.* If Bryan had secretly been cheating with Val and his other cheerleader floozies during our marriage, what else could he have kept from me? A violent streak? The urge to kill?

Suppose he's innocent. I turned the situation over in my head. *Who else might want Valentina dead?* She wasn't from the islands. Since my gut was telling me that her death wasn't a random incident, that meant the suspect pool could likely be confined to the only eight people here who knew her—aside from me, at least. Was it possible that one of Dante's other groomsmen was a cold-blooded killer? *Maybe Tom*, I thought. With his oversized biceps and mammoth hands, he could have crushed Val like a bug. Truthfully, any one of the fine-tuned football players would have had the strength to overpower her— but what could have been their motive for murder?

I turned my thoughts to the other women in the wedding party. The obvious choice was Coco Becker. While I couldn't fathom sweet Emma or mousy Mia being capable of such malice, Coco sure fit the bill. She'd been the best of pals with Valentina in public, but according to Mia, behind closed doors they'd been at each other's throats. It was no secret that Coco had been jealous of her cheer mate for landing my ex after they'd both hooked up with him. Now that her competition for his affection had been eliminated, perhaps she thought she could swoop in and win him over. She *had* wound up in Bryan's room awfully fast to comfort him. Was it because she'd already known that Val was dead before the rest of us had found her body?

There was also the fact that Coco hated me. She could've easily been the one to swipe my bag—she'd been at the club and on the bus with me the night before, giving her plenty of opportunity. Had she been the one to plant my purse on the corpse? Was the flighty cheerleader bit just an act? Deep down, was Coco diabolical enough to murder Val and set me up to take the fall?

So much for staying out of it, I thought glumly as I reached our room. Though I wanted nothing to do with the investigation into Val's mysterious death, if Detective Ray and his men were trying to build a case against me for the crime, I wasn't going to go down without a fight. I also couldn't stand idly by and let their case potentially ruin Emma's bachelorette weekend *and* keep her from making it home in time for her own wedding. I was going to have to do whatever it took to find out the truth about what happened to Valentina, both for my sake and Emma's.

I slid my key into the card slot on the door and pushed it open. The room was empty. Emma must have gone upstairs so Dante could console her, or perhaps she was next door with Mia. I walked over to the door that connected the two rooms and knocked softly. Mia opened it after a few seconds. She looked as exhausted as I felt. "This day has been a total nightmare," she said, and even her voice sounded tired. "Where have you been?"

"At the dress shop," I replied. "I dropped in to see my aunt and let her know that I was all right since word about what happened to Val has gotten around the resort." I left it at that, not wanting to divulge that I was being considered as a person of interest by the police. "Is Emma in there with you?" I asked, peeking over her shoulder.

Mia shook her head. "Upstairs with Dante. She's taking this all really hard." Mia's forehead wrinkled. "It's just so surreal," she said quietly. "I mean, one day Valentina is here, and the next..." She let her words hang in the air for a few moments and then dropped her gaze to the floor. "Do you want to come in?" she offered, stepping back and opening the door wider to let me through.

The room was a mirror image of the one I was sharing with Emma, with the same decor but the furniture arrangements reversed. "Is Coco here, too?" I asked, glancing around the dimly lit room. Mia had the curtains drawn, and one of the bedside lamps was the only source of light to illuminate the space, adding to the gloom.

Mia dropped onto one of the two beds. "Nope. I haven't seen her since before...well, before we went to the beach."

I crossed the room and hesitated next to the second bed, reluctant to sit on it knowing that one of its occupants was now dead. Instead, I perched on the love seat, folding my legs underneath me. "Did anything about Coco's behavior this morning strike you as a bit odd?" I asked, looking Mia in the eyes.

She cocked her head. "What do you mean?"

I shrugged. "You mentioned that she and Valentina were bickering in here last night before dinner, and then she didn't seem concerned when Val wasn't at breakfast this morning. It was almost as if she wasn't surprised when she didn't show up."

Mia was silent for a moment. "Maybe," she said finally. She rolled over on her stomach and propped herself up with her elbows. "I didn't notice anything unusual about the way she was acting at breakfast, but I guess I was still in a fog from last night." She frowned. "But now that you mention it, I do think it's pretty weird that she disappeared as soon as we found Val. I tried calling her when the police arrived, but she didn't answer her phone and still hasn't called me back." Her lower lip trembled. "I just thought she should hear about it from one of us, you know?" When I nodded my understanding, she continued. "I'm sure she knows by now—at least, I hope so." She looked up at me. "Where do you think she could have gone?"

"I actually saw her upstairs earlier," I admitted, choosing my words carefully. "I went to the guys' suite to make sure that someone had notified Bryan and the others, but she'd beaten me there. Tom answered the door." I grimaced. "He hates me. He wouldn't let me into the room, but I saw Coco in there, comforting Bryan."

"Oh." Mia's frown deepened. "Poor Bryan," she said softly.

"Coco went with Val to The Lava Pot last night, didn't she?" I asked, trying to get the conversation back on track. "Did they come back together?"

Mia shook her head. "I'm not even sure if Valentina came back at all. She headed straight for the bar as soon as we got off the party shuttle. Coco came in for a few minutes, but then she took off."

"Did she say where she was going?"

"No, but I assumed she went to join Val for a drink."

"So you were alone in the room?" I asked.

Mia shook her head again. "I might have had some company," she said, a sly grin spreading over her face.

I raised my head in surprise. "Really? Who?" Had she met a guy her first night on the island?

Her eyes sparkled. "You know Will, right? The hot groomsman with the sandy hair and perfect dimples?"

"Will Bolero?" I brightened. "That's great!" Of all of Bryan's teammates, I'd always liked him the best. He deserved to find a nice girl. "Will's such a sweet guy," I told her.

"And he's a great kisser too." Her smile widened, and her eyes got a dreamy, faraway look. I could tell she was completely smitten with the hunky placekicker.

"How did you two get together?" I asked.

Mia shrugged. "Oh, I don't know," she replied with a coy smile. "I mean, we're not dating or anything—not yet, at least. I met him through Emma, and we've been flirting back and forth for a while now. Then last night there was a knock on the door, and when I opened it, there he was. I was surprised to see him standing there—not that I'm complaining." She giggled.

"Oh. I see." I smiled in understanding. I glanced at the crumpled sheets on the other bed. "You said you're pretty sure Val never returned to the room, right? What about Coco?" I asked. "Were you and Will still awake when she came back?"

"No," she replied, stretching. "Will didn't stay the whole night, but he was here for a couple of hours. I went to sleep right after he left. I never heard anyone else come in, but when I woke up this morning, Coco was fast asleep in the other bed." She grimaced. "I didn't think anything was wrong when I didn't see Val anywhere. I just assumed she'd gotten up early to go for a jog on the beach or to hit the gym."

"You couldn't have known," I said, offering her what I hoped was a sympathetic look.

She nodded, giving me a strained smile. "Thanks." She stifled a yawn.

"I'll let you get some rest," I said, rising from the love seat. I had the feeling I'd already learned everything that Mia knew about Coco's whereabouts the night before. "I should see if I can find Emma."

I stepped around Coco's bed, pausing when I heard a soft crunching sound under my feet. I glanced down to find a light dusting of fine, white sand coating the carpet, along with a few tiny shards of broken seashells. Several thicker clumps formed a trail that led under the bed. We hadn't gone to the beach before leaving the resort for the Lanai Lounge the night before. That meant someone must have been out there last night and had tracked sand back into the room.

"What's wrong?" Mia asked, seeing me frown down at my feet.

I didn't answer. Crouching low, I lifted the comforter that was hanging over the side of the mattress. My heart gave a hard thump as I stared at the sparkly, black wedge sandals underneath the bed, their soles caked with sand. The strappy shoes belonged to Coco.

CHAPTER SEVEN

———

"Wasn't Coco wearing these last night?" I asked, trying to tamp down the excitement mounting in my chest.

Mia rose from the other bed and stooped down beside me. "Yeah," she replied, nodding. "I remember because I complimented her on them. They're super cute, huh?"

I lifted one of the sandals for closer inspection. The same powdery sand dusted the straps, and there were tiny fragments of broken shells wedged into the grooves of the rubber soles. *Bingo.* Thanks to Mia, I now knew that Coco had left the room, allegedly in search of Valentina. Had she caught up with her frenemy at the bar and then lured her to her doom on the beach? I felt hope bloom in my chest. *Could this be my first real lead?*

The door to the room suddenly flew open. Startled, I dropped the sandal back onto the floor and kicked it under the bed just as Coco appeared in the doorway. She stepped into the room and paused, casting me an annoying look. "What are *you* doing here?"

Play nice, I thought. Now was a good time to see if I could get a read on her. "Mia and I were just talking about what happened to Valentina. I'm so sorry, Coco," I said, giving her what I hoped was a sincere look. "I know you two were close."

The busty cheerleader narrowed her eyes. "Are you really sorry?" She stomped across the room and flung herself onto the bed. "You hated her," she said, rolling over so that her back was to me. "For all we know, you're the one who killed her." She twisted her body so that she was facing me again, her eyes blazing with accusation. "And then you sent the cops after Bryan to throw suspicion off yourself."

Mia turned and gawked at me. "You did?"

I sucked in a breath. "I didn't mean for the police to go after him," I said, forcing an even tone. "The detective asked me for the names of everyone who traveled here with Valentina. I had no choice but to tell him about everyone in the wedding party—including Bryan." I clasped my hands in front of me to keep from fidgeting. "Valentina and I didn't get along, but I wouldn't have wished for something like this to happen. I really hope they catch whoever killed her."

"Why didn't you call me back, Coco?" Mia asked, pulling herself into a seated position on the other bed. "Emma and I tried to find you after the police came. We were worried about you."

Coco sat up on the bed. She casually shrugged one shoulder but avoided Mia's gaze. "I was flirting with that sexy lifeguard," she said smugly. "He totally wanted me, but I decided he wasn't really my type."

I felt a smirk tug at one corner of my lips. I knew for a fact that Remy hadn't been interested in Coco. He was only attracted to male bodybuilders.

"Anyway, I didn't feel like going out to the beach, so I went upstairs to see what the guys were up to," Coco continued. Her arrogant smile faded. "That's when I found out about Val," she said quietly, a slight tremble in her words.

I studied her closely. Was the grief in her expression just an act? "Did you go to the tiki bar to meet up with Val when we got back to the resort last night?" I pressed. "What happened there?"

Coco narrowed her eyes in mistrust. "Why are you asking so many questions?" she demanded. "I came back here for a nap, not an interrogation." She rose from the bed and stormed across the room. "But since that's obviously not going to happen, I'm going for a walk." Coco turned around to give me the stink eye one last time. "And it'd be great if you weren't here when I get back, Kaley." She stepped out into the hallway and slammed the door loudly behind her.

I exchanged a glance with Mia. "I didn't mean to agitate her," I said, shrugging.

Mia gave a dismissive wave. "Don't worry about it. Just give her a little time to cool off. She's upset. We all are." She placed a hand over her mouth to stifle another yawn. "A nap does sound like a good idea, though," she said, settling back onto the bed and resting her head on one of the fluffy pillows.

I said goodbye to Mia and ducked back into Emma's and my room, trying to decide my next move. I wasn't sure when Emma would return, and I couldn't stand the thought of sitting in there alone while my name was getting dragged through the mud with the local homicide department. I decided to use the free time to follow up on Valentina's last whereabouts before she'd been killed. If she'd actually made it to The Lava Pot, perhaps someone else who'd been there last night had seen something. I decided it couldn't hurt to go grab a cocktail and see what information I could dig up. I quickly changed out of my bathing suit and cover-up, donning a pair of khaki shorts and a navy blue halter top. I left a note on the resort stationery for Emma to let her know I'd be back soon and then set off for The Lava Pot.

Even in the midafternoon, the little beachfront tiki bar was teeming with activity. Guests were crowded around the counter, barking their drink orders to the tall, blond bartender. I took a seat at the opposite end of the bar and waited patiently for several minutes. When the rush died down, I held up a hand to catch the man's attention.

He regarded me with a courteous smile. "What can I get you, love?" he asked in a charming British accent.

"Hi, Casey," I said, reading his name tag. "I'd like a Blue Hawaiian, if it's not too much trouble." My hangover was long gone, and the stress of the morning had left me in need of a drink. Plus, sitting at the bar and enjoying a cocktail gave me an excuse to chat him up and see if he knew anything.

"Of course." He flashed me his pearly whites before turning around to grab a bottle of Blue Curacao off the shelf.

"Mind if I ask you a few questions?" I called, leaning over the counter so he could hear me over the chatter.

He shrugged. "Sure. Just a sec." Casey tended to another couple who had wandered up to order some daiquiris. When he was done, he returned to my corner of the bar. "You're Noa's girlfriend, right?" he asked, cocking his head as he looked me over.

I bobbed my head in what I hoped was a noncommittal manner. We hadn't exactly reached the stage for labels just yet. "I'm Kaley," I told him. "I work over in the Happy Hula Dress Boutique."

"Nice to meet you, Kaley," he said with a smile that showed off his dimples. "What's on your mind?"

"I'm sure you've heard about the body they found on the beach this morning," I began.

Casey cringed. "Right. It's practically all that anyone has been talking about today. The police came by earlier to speak to the few of us who were working last night."

"You were here last night?" I tried not to sound too eager.

He nodded. "The poor girl who was murdered came in about an hour before closing," he said, grabbing a clean rag from beneath the counter and beginning to wipe the surface. "I think one of the other bartenders served her a couple of Shark Bites." He grimaced. "I'd have turned her away if she'd tried to order from me—she already seemed rather snockered."

"Was she here alone?" I asked. When Casey gave me a curious look, I decided I'd better explain myself. "The girl who was killed—Valentina—came to the resort with a close friend of mine. As you can imagine, my friend is distraught about Val's death. I'm just trying to find out what happened in hopes of giving her some closure."

"I see. Doing a little detective work of your own?" Casey's lips twitched, and there was a faint twinkle in his eye that told me perhaps he had some experience in that department himself.

"Caught me," I said, holding up my hands in mock surrender. I sipped my drink while I regained my composure. In a more serious tone, I repeated my question. "So, *was* Valentina alone?"

"As a matter of fact, no." Casey set the rag down and propped his elbows on the counter.

"Really?" I leaned forward in anticipation. Was he about to confirm that Coco had met up with Val at the little bar?

Casey lowered his voice. "She sat in the corner, over there," he said, inclining his head to a table on the other side of the bar. "With a blond fellow."

"A guy?" My eyebrows rose. *Not Coco after all.*

"He was tall, about my height, though maybe a bit more muscular."

Something stirred in my gut. *Bryan.* "How were they acting?" I pressed on, feeling my pulse quicken.

He shrugged. "They appeared to be arguing about something. They both stayed until last call. After that, they took off in separate directions."

I frowned. What had they been fighting about? Had Bryan really gone away on his own, or had he followed Valentina out to the beach, where their argument had taken a deadly turn? *And what about Coco?*

"You didn't happen to see a petite woman with bleached blonde hair come in around the same time they were here, did you?" I asked. I held one hand level with my chin. "About this tall, busty, with a face that looks like she's constantly sucking on a lemon?"

Casey's jaw went slack. "As a matter of fact, yes," he said. "That's a pretty spot-on description." He glanced around the bar. Seeming satisfied that no one was listening, he continued. "It was strange. She sat at the bar alone and ordered a few rounds from me. She appeared to have a keen interest in your friend and her beau—she barely took her eyes off them the entire time she was here. When they left, she was quick to pay her own tab and then scurried after them."

"She never spoke to them?"

Casey shook his head. "I don't think so. She never got up from the bar, and I'm not even sure if they saw her. Every time I looked their way, they seemed rather wrapped up in their argument."

Interesting. Bryan had been the last person to be seen with Valentina before she'd been murdered, but it sounded as if Coco may have been stalking them. Had my ex-hubby attacked his girlfriend on the beach, or had Coco lured her out there after the couple had parted ways?

"You told all of this to the police?" I asked.

"Every word," Casey replied.

I placed a tip in his jar. "Thank you. You've been very helpful." I took a sip of my drink. "And this is delicious, by the way."

His eyes twinkled again. "My pleasure, love. Cheers." He gave me a slight bow before walking to the other end of the bar to attend to another thirsty guest.

I finished my drink and rose from the stool, feeling a bit more optimistic about my future. If Casey really had told the police the same story he'd just shared with me, surely Detective Ray would have to shift his attention to Bryan or Coco. *Wouldn't he?*

I thought about it for a few moments. My gut didn't seem convinced. I'd seen the burly homicide detective and his team fixate on the wrong suspect before. To be safe, I'd have to continue digging for the truth on my own. There was no turning back now—I was officially on the case.

CHAPTER EIGHT

———

Friday evening was uneventful. Emma returned from spending time with Dante and headed to bed early, insisting that all she wanted to do was sleep. With our snorkeling plans canceled, Mia took off to see what Will and the other groomsmen were up to. Coco kept to herself in her room, and I didn't bother trying to speak with her again, thinking it best to give the not-so-cheerful cheerleader some time to cool off before I made another attempt to pry any information from her. After all, thanks to my trip to The Lava Pot, I already had my suspicions that she'd been stalking Valentina at the bar and that Bryan may have been the last person to be seen with the doomed woman while she was still alive—unless there was a witness somewhere on the resort who had spotted Val with Coco after my ex-hubby had returned to his suite.

Though I thought my next move should be to speak to Bryan, I'd unfortunately have to wait until I could get him away from Tom—assuming Bry would even speak to me now that he probably knew I'd been the one to send Detective Ray up to his room. Instead, I spent my evening at the pool bar with Jamie, sharing my theories about Val's murder.

"My money's on Bryan," she said between sips of her mango daiquiri. "He *was* seen with her right before she was murdered, and the bartender even said he saw them arguing." She shrugged. "Seems pretty open and shut, if you ask me."

"Not necessarily," I countered. "Coco stalked Val to The Lava Pot, and when I tried to ask her what happened after that, she totally shut me down. Then there are the sandy shoes under her bed. What are the odds that Coco decided to go for a solo moonlight stroll by the shore at the same time that Valentina was being murdered on the very same beach?"

"Fair point," Jamie said. "Still, does Bryan have a supposed alibi?"

I took a pull from my own daiquiri. "I'm hoping to ask him if I can ever get past Tom 'The Brick Wall' Evans." I made a face.

"You'll figure something out," she said, playfully chucking me on the shoulder. Her phone dinged, and I saw her eyes light up as she scanned the message on the screen.

"Who's that?" I asked, unable to hide my curiosity. "New guy?"

"Maybe," Jamie replied, her attention still fixed on her phone. Her lips lifted at the corners.

"You didn't tell me you had a new boyfriend."

"Who said anything about boyfriends?" Jamie wagged a finger at me.

"Yeah, yeah." I gave a dismissive wave and leaned over and tried to peek at her phone screen. "Anyone I know?"

"Maybe," Jamie said again, though she avoided my gaze.

I jokingly reached for her phone. "Oh, come on. Who is it?"

She pushed my hand away. "Remember that cute bouncer from the club last night?" she asked, grinning.

My eyebrows reached for the sky. "Javi? How'd he get your number?"

She winked. "I slipped it to him on our way out."

"Very nice." I nodded my approval. "So you two are…?"

"Just texting right now," she supplied, though her smile widened. "But he *did* just ask if I'd like to get dinner with him at the Loco Moco tonight before his shift at the Lanai Lounge."

I clapped my hands together. "Go for it! Javi's the best. He and Noa are really great friends." I let out an excited little cheer. "Ooh! We could go on double dates."

"Whoa. Slow down, Speedy Gonzales." Jamie set her phone on the counter and held up her hands. "It's just dinner. Don't start planning the wedding just yet." She slurped down the rest of her drink and slid off the barstool. "I told him I'd meet him in half an hour, so I should go freshen up. I'll see you tomorrow at the spa." She grinned again. "I'm overdue for a mani-pedi."

"You and me both." I pushed my own drink aside. "Have fun," I called as I watched Jamie saunter away from the bar. I hopped off the stool and headed back to the room, slipping into bed and pulling the comforter up to my chin.

I'd hoped to fall asleep at a decent hour since I'd promised to meet Noa early the next morning to go buy my new phone, but my mind just wouldn't turn off. I lay awake in bed for hours, picturing Bryan and Valentina sitting a secluded corner of The Lava Pot while Coco spied on them from the bar counter. I puzzled over why she hadn't just gone up to their table. Had she not wanted to be seen? Why not? I tried to envision Coco stalking the couple as they left the bar. Maybe she was just a sad, lonely girl, drowning her sorrows in a drink while she watched her crush give his affection to another woman. *Or maybe she was jealous enough to kill her competition,* I thought, remembering her sandy shoes.

But Bryan and Val were fighting, the voice in my head argued. Casey the bartender had said that he'd seen them part ways when they left The Lava Pot, but could he have been mistaken? Maybe he'd only thought he saw Bryan leave Valentina alone. *Or maybe Bryan just didn't want any witnesses,* I thought. Perhaps he'd stormed off in the opposite direction of Val, knowing that others at the bar might be watching them. Could he have doubled back and followed her out to the beach?

Despite all of the scenarios swirling around in my head, I finally managed to drift off to sleep. I awoke just after dawn on Saturday morning. After a quick shower, I got dressed and sneaked out of the room. I was relieved that Emma finally seemed to be sleeping peacefully as I headed for the door. I'd heard her fitfully tossing and turning several times throughout the night. The poor thing had to be exhausted. Careful not to wake her, I slipped out of the room as quietly as I could and gently pulled the door closed behind me.

As promised, I found Noa waiting for me on one of the benches in the courtyard. He was dressed in blue board shorts and a fitted black V-neck, his long, dark hair knotted in a bun atop his head—a style choice that I often teased him about.

"How's my favorite hipster?" I joked, lightly tapping his man bun as I sat down beside him.

Noa wagged a finger at me, a look of mock disappointment on his face. "If you're going to poke fun at me, maybe I shouldn't give you the surprise I brought for you."

Ooh. I liked surprises. "Okay, okay," I said, laughing. "I'm sorry." I scooted closer to him. "What is it?"

Noa reached down for something he'd tucked beneath the bench. "I know we made plans to go pick up a replacement phone for you this morning," he began, handing me a plastic shopping bag with my phone carrier's logo on it. "But I had some free time after my shift yesterday, so I went ahead and dropped by the shop. I know the manager, and I got your account password on the second guess." He winked. "You should really consider using something other than your birthday."

I pulled the bag open and gaped down at the brand-new iPhone still inside the box. "These things cost a fortune," I sputtered. I shoved the bag back at Noa, feeling embarrassed. "I can't afford this."

"You were overdue for an upgrade," he replied, pushing it toward me again. "And, like I said, I know the manager—I taught his son how to surf last year for free. He gave me his employee discount." He grinned. "I also had him sync all of your backed-up contacts from the cloud, so all you have to do is turn the phone on and you're ready to roll."

I pulled the phone out of the box and lightly ran my fingertips over the smooth surface. "You didn't have to do all that," I said softly.

Noa shrugged. "After the hectic day you had yesterday, I wanted to do something to make you smile."

I felt my mouth tug up at the corners. "You're so thoughtful," I said, squeezing his hand. "It's one of the things I love about you." As soon as the words left my lips, I was hit with a jolt of panic. *Oh no.* I hadn't meant to say the big *L* word. We weren't even officially in a relationship yet! Afraid to look over at him, I dropped my gaze to my hands. "Er, thanks again for doing that," I said quickly, hoping my tone didn't betray how mortified I was. "I'll find a way to return the favor. Maybe a seat upgrade or a few drinks on the flight back from Atlanta."

Noa went tense beside me. "That's not necessary," he said gruffly. "You don't owe me anything." I glanced over just as he looked down at his watch. "Sorry, but I've got to go, Kales. I want to knock out a web design mock-up for a new client by tomorrow, and I've got my work cut out for me." He rose quickly from the bench and stooped down to plant a chaste kiss on my forehead. "I'll call you later, 'kay?"

"Okay," I said, though at that moment all I wanted was to sink through the bench. I watched him hurry off as if he couldn't get away from me fast enough. Then I did a mental face palm. Noa and I had only been seeing each other for a few weeks, and I'd been divorced for barely three times that. The word had just slipped out, and rather than clarifying what I'd actually meant, I'd panicked.

While what I'd been trying to say was that I loved his *thoughtfulness,* what if he'd taken my accidental L-bomb to mean that I was becoming too attached to him? I thought back over the previous week, at Noa's aloofness every time I'd brought up the topic of taking him to Atlanta as my date to Emma's wedding. If he'd considered that to be moving too fast, then this must have really thrown him for a loop. No wonder he'd bolted at the first opportunity.

I pressed the power button on my new phone, staring glumly down at the screen while it booted. I was surprised when it immediately buzzed with a new notification. There was a voice mail from a local number. It was time-stamped from yesterday afternoon. Curious, I clicked on the little icon and held the phone up to my ear as the recorded message began to play. "Hi, Kaley. It's Gabby LeClair from Gabby's Island Adventures. I'm returning your call regarding a missing purse. Koma found a black bag on our bus that matches the description you left in your message. I just wanted to let you know that I'm holding it for you in my office whenever you'd like to come pick it up."

I replayed the recording once more, certain I'd heard Gabby wrong. My purse had been found with Valentina's corpse. *Could she be talking about Val's bag?* I wondered. Maybe no one had planted my purse on the body to try to frame me for the crime. Perhaps the deceased woman had simply grabbed my purse by mistake. It *had* been dark on the bus, and she'd been pretty intoxicated. It would have been easy to confuse the two bags.

Maybe there's something in Valentina's purse that might point to her killer. It was a long shot, but I was willing to explore any and all possibilities.

A new wave of hope lifted through me as I rose from the bench and hurried back into the resort lobby, headed in the direction of Gabby's Island Adventures. The little travel agency was located past the concierge's desk and close to the resort gift shop. I found the owner, Gabby LeClair, seated at one of two rattan desks. She smiled brightly when I walked in.

"Good morning, Gabby," I said. "I just got your voice mail and happened to be right around the corner."

"Hi, Kaley." Gabby rose from her chair, lifting a hand to smooth the dark streak that ran through her mostly blonde hair as she walked over to give me a hug. She pulled away and glanced in the direction of the other desk, where a dark-haired young woman was busy typing away at her keyboard. "Lana, could you please get the purse that Koma found on the shuttle?"

The younger woman looked up and nodded. She smiled at me as she got up from her desk and disappeared behind the partition that separated the women's workspaces from the rest of the little office.

When Lana was gone, Gabby returned her attention to me. Her eyes crinkled, and she gave me a sympathetic look. "I was so sorry to hear about your friend. Is it true you found the poor woman?" she asked, lowering her voice. When I nodded, she drew in a breath. "That must have been awful." There was a hint of sad understanding in her tone. I'd heard talk around the resort that she'd had her fair share of bad luck in the dead body department. "If there's anything I can do for you, just ask," she added, squeezing my arm.

"Thanks." I smiled to show my gratitude.

Lana emerged from the back, carrying a black leather satchel that looked very similar to the one that Emma had given me. "Here's your bag," she said, holding out the strap so that I could take it.

"*My* bag," I repeated, holding it against my chest. I glanced from Lana to Gabby. Both women looked back at me with neutral expressions. Was this some kind of trick, or did they really not know about my purse being found with Valentina's body? This had to be the first time the resort gossip mill had skipped over one of the juicy details. I felt a nervous heat begin to creep up my collarbone. *Just in case, I'd better get out of here before they realize their mistake.*

I slipped the purse strap over my shoulder and made a show of glancing at my watch. "I've got to meet a friend for brunch," I said, backing toward the door. I thanked both Lana and Gabby before forcing myself to walk calmly out the door. I kept walking until I was out of sight of the little agency's office.

I stopped and leaned against the wall of the lobby, not sure what to do next. I knew the right thing would be to turn the purse in to the police, which meant I should call Detective Ray. Still, it wouldn't hurt to give it a quick look-through first, would it? If there was something inside Val's purse that could provide a lead, I had to know. My mind made up, I turned down the nearest hallway and ducked into the ladies' room, murmuring a polite hello to a pair of elderly women standing at the sinks. I slipped into one of the empty stalls and then unzipped the bag's main compartment.

Every time I'd seen Valentina, she'd always seemed impeccably put together, not a single stray hair or clumpy eyelash. The inside of her purse, however, looked like a glitter bomb had gone off. Shimmery makeup particles dusted the contents of the bag, and I coughed as the strong smell of Val's perfume assaulted my nostrils. Her wallet, hairbrush, and a tube of *Retro Ruby*–hued lipstick were nestled on a bed of crumpled receipts and loose change. There was one item noticeably absent from the bag, however: Val's cell phone. *Did she have her phone with her when she was killed?* I wondered.

I plucked Valentina's wallet from the top of the pile and flipped it open, shoving away the flicker of jealousy when I saw her weight and height next to her flawless driver's license photo. Opening her billfold, I was taken aback by the thick stack of money inside. Though it was a glamorous job, I knew from my time as a football wife that being a cheerleader for the NFL paid next to nothing. *So, what was Valentina doing to earn so much cash?* I wondered as I thumbed through the fat pile of bills. Had

Bryan given her the money? He could certainly afford to be her sugar daddy—he'd been the one to keep the millions when we'd gone our separate ways, thanks to an ironclad prenuptial agreement that, unfortunately for me, hadn't included an infidelity clause.

Using a wad of toilet paper, I wiped my prints from the wallet and then dropped it back into the dead woman's purse. Instinctively, I grabbed the handful of crinkled receipts from the bottom of the bag and unfurled them one by one, scanning the contents. There were three fast food order slips and a receipt for a two-liter of Diet Coke and two bags of cookies from Walmart.

How did Val wolf down so many Oreos and Taco Bell burritos and still look like a super model? I wondered. I dropped the four receipts back into the bag. It was unfair that she could inhale so much junk food and still rock a perfect figure, but that was hardly a reason for either Bryan or Coco to have killed her.

There was one last crumpled slip of paper. I opened it and read over the text at the very top. It was a receipt from a pharmacy in Midtown Atlanta called Peachtree Drugs. I recognized the name—the little store was located on the corner across Peachtree Street from the condo building where Bryan lived. There was a time stamp on the receipt from ten thirty on Wednesday night, just three days ago. According to the readout, Val had purchased a bottle of Vitamin water, a box of antacids, and…

A sudden shock tore through me. I sat down hard on the toilet seat, my head swimming as I reread the small print in disbelief.

The last item on the receipt was a pregnancy test.

CHAPTER NINE

———

    I sat in the bathroom stall for what felt like an eternity, struggling to catch my breath as I stared at the drugstore receipt. *A pregnancy test.* The words repeated in my mind like a broken record. Could Valentina have really been pregnant? If so, the receipts for all the junk food would certainly make a lot more sense.

    She was drinking at the Lanai Lounge on Thursday night, I thought, frowning. *Wasn't she?* I strained to recall the events of the night in question, but I couldn't remember actually seeing Val down a cocktail or shot. I'd been ignoring her for the most part, focusing on Emma and making sure she was enjoying her big night out. Was it possible that Valentina had only pretended to get drunk along with the rest of us to cover up her secret?

    Or maybe the test was negative, I tried to reassure myself. I'd taken my fair share of EPTs in the past only to find out that I didn't actually have a bun in the oven. Maybe Val had just had a little pregnancy scare and I was jumping to conclusions. *But what if the test* was *positive?* A horrible realization struck me, making me heartsick. If that were the case, it would make Val's murder a double homicide.

    Would Bryan know? I couldn't just come out and ask him without raising his suspicions about how I might have found out. *And if he didn't know…* My heart clenched. I couldn't bring myself to be the bearer of that devastating news, especially if it might not even be true.

    Feeling numb, I stuffed the receipt back into the purse and then hugged the bag to my chest. I sat quietly for several more moments, trying to compose myself. When my breathing finally returned to normal, I forced myself out of the bathroom stall. I had to call Detective Ray. I didn't know how long autopsies took, but if Val had really been pregnant, it was only a matter of time before the truth came to light. In the meantime, I couldn't tell the detective my suspicions about Val's condition, but I could turn in the purse and hope that he read the receipts and came to the same conclusion that I had.

Retrieving my new phone from my tote bag, I dialed the Aloha Lagoon Police Department as I returned to the resort lobby. The operator patched me through to Detective Ray's office line, but he didn't answer. "Detective, this is Kaley Kalua," I said to his answering machine. "I found something that might help with your investigation into the murder of Valentina Cruz. Please call me back when you get this. I'll be at the resort."

I had just ended the call and slipped my phone back into my tote when I heard someone calling my name from across the lobby.

"Hey, Kaley!" I looked up to find a familiar dark-skinned man with long dreadlocks standing next to a tall, muscular blond man near the entrance to the Loco Moco Café.

"Hey," I called back, waving to two of Dante's groomsmen, Freddy Jenkins and Will Bolero. I slung the purse onto my shoulder alongside my tote and closed the gap between us. I forced what I hoped was a cheerful smile. Until I talked to Bryan and determined if he'd known about Val's potential condition, I didn't want his friends to suspect anything was amiss—aside from the obvious, of course. "How are you two holding up?" I asked, hesitating for a moment before adding, "How is Bryan?"

Will gave a rueful shake of his head. "Rough. He's completely shut down. Bry's barely spoken a word since he got the news."

"That's awful," I murmured, though I felt my suspicion rise. I'd supported Bryan through grief before, and he'd never been the type to suffer in silence. My ex-husband was very vocal about his personal life, using everything from triumphs to tragedies as a ploy for more publicity. When his father had passed away last year, Bryan had almost missed the funeral after booking an interview at the same time as the service. Could the uncharacteristic stoicism mean that he was hiding something?

"Have you eaten?" Will asked. "Why don't you join us for breakfast? My treat." He hiked his thumb over his shoulder in the direction of the café. "Dante went to check on Emma, but Tom and Bryan grabbed a table out on the patio. I'm sure we could make room for one more."

I chewed the inside of my lip. It would be hard to seek out Bryan's alibi in front of his teammates, but I wasn't sure when I'd have another opportunity to speak to him. "Thanks," I said, flashing a smile at the two men.

Freddy led the way through the bustling café, and I fell into step beside Will. I pulled my sunglasses down over my eyes as we stepped out onto the bright patio. Adjusting the collar of my blue top, I strode purposefully toward the table where Bryan and Tom were already seated, sipping glasses of pineapple iced tea.

"Look who we found in the lobby," Will said. He dragged an extra chair over from the closest empty table and gestured for me to have a seat between Freddy and him. I smiled to show my gratitude.

Tom rose from his chair, the hard look in his eyes giving me the impression that he was ready to boot me from the table. Bryan held up a hand, and the big man grudgingly sat back down.

"Hi, Kaley," my ex said quietly.

"Hi," I replied in a soft voice, steeling myself against the barrage of emotions that suddenly welled up in my chest. Aside from our brief encounter at the airport, this was the first time I'd been face-to-face with my ex-husband since I'd moved across the continent to get away from him. While part of me still wanted to scream and throw things at him, I couldn't help but feel sorry for his loss. And there was another part of me still that wasn't convinced he'd had nothing to do with Val's death.

Remember why you're here, my inner voice piped up. I plastered what I hoped was a look of sincerity on my face as I met Bryan's gaze. "I'm really sorry about Val," I said, and I meant it.

"Thanks," he mumbled. A wave of sympathy rolled through me at the hollow sound of his voice.

"Are you sorry you sicced the police on us?" Tom asked gruffly. I looked over to find him still glowering at me from across the table.

My shoulders stiffened. "I couldn't just lie to the police and pretend you guys weren't here," I fired back defensively. "The detective asked me for the names of everyone from the wedding party that was staying at the resort. I didn't have a choice." I looked to Will and Freddy for backup, but they both avoided my gaze.

"It's all right." To my surprise, it was Bryan who came to my rescue. "You did what you had to do, Kaley. Nobody's blaming you for anything."

"Speak for yourself," Tom said belligerently.

"Cool it, Evans," Bryan snapped. His jaw clenched, and one of the veins in his neck began to throb. "Excuse me," he said, abruptly rising from the table. "I need a minute." He stalked toward the edge of the patio and stepped out into the sand.

Tom rose, too. "I told you to leave him alone," he said, glaring at me before taking off after his buddy.

I watched them go and then let out a frustrated breath. I should have known I wouldn't be able to talk to Bryan with Tom around.

"Don't let Big T get to you," Freddy said, catching my eye. "He has a hard time leaving his job on the field."

I nodded. Not only did Tom protect Bryan and the other running backs on the field, but now he'd charged himself with running emotional defense for my ex, too. I couldn't fault him for following his instincts—after all, he had a right to be wary of me, considering I was there to try to determine Bryan's possible involvement in his girlfriend's murder.

"How are *you* hanging in there, Kaley?" Freddy asked. "You're the one who found Val on the beach, right?"

"Yeah," I said lamely, not sure what else to say. After a pause, I added, "Mia and Emma were there too."

"Yikes." Will's mouth set in a grim line. He reached across the table and took my hand, squeezing it gently. The gesture went a long way toward putting me at ease. "I'm sorry you had to go through that. It must have been pretty traumatic."

I grimaced. *You have no idea.*

"How did she die?" Freddy asked.

It was an odd question, and my gaze snapped to him. "Huh?"

Freddy gave me a sheepish look. "Sorry. Morbid curiosity, I guess. I just wondered if you could tell what happened." He leaned forward, watching me with an intent expression.

"Come on, man," Will groaned. He ran a hand over his close-cropped hair. "That's messed up."

I held up a hand. "It's okay," I told Will. I pushed my sunglasses back on top of my hair and looked from one man to the other. "I'm not sure how she died," I said honestly. I swallowed, picturing the blood darkening the sand beneath her temple. "But I think it might have been a head wound of some kind—like maybe someone hit her with something." My brows pinched. "But who could have done something like that? And why?"

Freddy laced his hands behind his head, his expression turning thoughtful. "Well, I don't know if this is relevant since we're all the way across the country, but there is one guy who comes to mind that might have wanted to hurt Val. She had a stalker for a while back in Atlanta."

I felt a visceral tug in my gut, and my ears perked. "A stalker?"

Freddy exchanged a glance with Will and then met my eyes. "There was this guy," he said, shooting a furtive look over his shoulder toward Bryan and Tom. They were still standing near the edge of the patio, arguing. Freddy faced me again and lifted a menu to shield his face from their view. He lowered his voice. "So, a few weeks ago, I spotted Valentina heading to her car when I was leaving practice. There was this dude following her—like, he was obviously watching her, and when she got into her car, homeboy hopped in one a few rows over and followed her out of the parking lot. I went back to the locker room and told Bryan about what I saw. He got all huffy but said he'd handle it. The next morning at practice, I asked him if he'd managed to catch up to the guy. All he would tell me was that Val was all right and that I shouldn't worry about it."

Goosebumps pricked my arms. The idea of an obsessive stranger following Val around gave me the creeps. "Did you ever find out who the guy was?" I asked.

Freddy shrugged. "No clue. Bryan never mentioned him again, and I didn't ask Valentina about it. I didn't want to freak her out."

"My guess is that he was just some overzealous fan," Will said. "Some guy with a thing for cheerleaders, maybe." He shrugged. "At least it seems like Bryan chased him off before things could escalate."

But what if he didn't? I wondered, darting a look at Bryan, who was heading back toward the table with Tom. What if Val's stalker had followed her to Aloha Lagoon?

"Don't ask him about it," Freddy whispered just before the two men reached the table. "He's got enough on his mind. There's no point in upsetting him further, right?"

I nodded my understanding.

"Sorry about that," Bryan mumbled as he dropped back into his chair. He avoided my gaze by picking up one of the menus and perusing the first page.

Tom took a seat beside him. Though he said nothing, his eyes fixed on me, narrowed with mistrust.

"It's okay," I told Bryan. "I didn't mean to cause any trouble. I just wanted to pay my condolences." I swallowed. "I know we're not on the best of terms"—okay, so that was a massive understatement—"but I really am sorry for your loss."

"Thanks." Bryan rubbed his hand over his face. He sighed. "I know it's early, but I could sure use a stiff drink." He lifted a hand to flag the nearest server.

Seeing my window of opportunity, I pounced on it. "They only serve a handful of premixed drinks here at the café," I told him. "Though if you want a specialty cocktail, the wait staff can run over to The Lava Pot and have the bartender whip one up—once they open, that is." I made a show of glancing around the table, making eye contact with each of the guys. Everyone except Tom, anyway. "Have any of you dropped by

The Lava Pot yet? They serve some of the best drinks on the island."

Freddy shook his head.

"Nope," Will replied.

Bryan didn't answer, and out of the corner of my eye, I saw his shoulders stiffen. When I tried to look him in the face, he turned away from me. "Screw it," he said, rising from the table. He reached in his pocket and pulled out his wallet, tossing a couple of bills onto the table next to his iced tea. "I'll just go upstairs and grab something from the mini bar." He started to turn away from the table but paused, lowering his shades. His gazed was fixed just past my shoulder. "Huh," he muttered, a frown creasing his face. "Your purse looks just like Val's."

"What?" My stomach dropped as three other pairs of eyes shifted toward the bag hoisted over my shoulder. It hadn't occurred to me that Bryan might recognize it. I had to give the purse to Detective Ray as potential evidence—so I couldn't let my ex-hubby know that it really did belong to his girlfriend. "Oh, this?" I said, trying to sound nonchalant. "I got it from the boutique where I work." I gave them what I thought was a breezy smile as I discreetly adjusted the purse so that it was obscured from view by my large tote bag. "Employees get a hefty discount—one of the perks of the job."

"That's nice," Bryan said, though I couldn't tell from his tone whether or not he believed me.

I was literally saved by the bell as my new phone sang out from the depths of my tote. "Just a sec," I murmured, riffling through the bag until I located it and tapped at the screen. There was a new message from Emma:

Emergency!

My heart gave a lurch. Maybe *saved* had been the wrong word. "You stay," I told Bryan, rising quickly to my feet. "I'll go. Emma needs me."

"Is everything all right?" Freddy asked.

I gave a little wave. "I'm sure it's fine. Probably just wedding planning duties. Nothing the maid of honor can't fix." I said goodbye to the guys and made my way back through the café. As I hurried out into the lobby, I nearly collided with a man who suddenly stepped into my path. I gave a startled cry and jumped back.

"Oh! Gosh, I'm so sorry, ma'am," the man drawled in a Southern accent. "I should pay more attention to where I'm walking."

"It's all right," I replied, flustered. I eyed the man curiously. He was of average height with a round frame and chubby face hidden behind several days' worth of graying stubble. His beady green eyes sized me up in turn, his thin smile suggesting that he liked what he saw. Something about the man seemed vaguely familiar, though I couldn't place it. *Must be the accent*, I thought, trying to shake off the icky vibe he was giving off. *Reminds me of the South is all.*

I excused myself and stepped around the man, dialing Emma's number as I walked briskly through the lobby. "I just got your text," I said as soon as she answered. "What's the emergency?"

"Oh, Kaley. I don't know what to do!" she wailed.

"Do about what?" I demanded. "Em, what's wrong? Where are you?"

It was no use. The rest of her words sounded like unintelligible groaning mixed with sobs. Consumed by worry, I dropped my phone back into my bag and quickened my pace. I rounded the corner to the first hallway of rooms, making a beeline toward our door. Stepping inside, I found Emma huddled in Dante's arms on the love seat, sobbing into his sleeve as Mia and Coco looked on with twin looks of pity.

"What happened?" I demanded. I could feel my heart pounding in my throat as I rushed to Emma's side.

She looked up at me and wiped her eyes. "Detective Ray called," she said, her voice quavering under the weight of her tears. "He said that until they get to the bottom of what happened to Valentina, he doesn't want anyone from the wedding party to leave the island." She began to cry all over again. "We have to cancel our flight home tomorrow, which means we won't make it back to Atlanta in time for the ceremony. Our wedding is ruined."

CHAPTER TEN

———

My heart sank. Noa had been right—and I'd been so wrapped up in trying to prevent this very thing from happening that I hadn't even thought to warn Emma that it was a possibility.

"Oh, Em," I murmured. "I'm so sorry. I wish there was something I could do." I chewed my lip, looking from my distraught friend to her somber fiancé, trying to think of how I could possibly fix their predicament. The only way to clear the wedding party to leave the island would be to catch Valentina's killer.

Coco stepped forward. "Don't worry, Em," she cooed, grabbing the other woman's hand. "I'll help you call all the guests and let them know we're postponing the ceremony. I'm sure it'll only be by a couple of days at most." She cast a snide look in my direction. "And if Kaley can't get off work to fly to Atlanta, I'm happy to step up and be your maid of honor. We *are* about to be family, after all."

Emma sighed. "Thanks for the offer, Coco. I just wish there was some way we could get to the wedding on time."

"Wait a minute." An idea came to me in a brilliant flash, and I snapped my fingers. "If you can't make it home for your wedding, why not bring the wedding to you?"

Emma dabbed at her eyes again and looked up at me, blinking. "Huh?" She glanced at Dante, who looked equally confused.

I grinned. "What if the two of you got married right here on the island?" I began to pace the room as I worked through my plan in my head. "There are several chapels near the resort—or we could even hold a private cliffside ceremony." Ideas were sparking through my mind so fast that I could barely spit them all out. "My friend Jimmy is close with a photographer here on the island—and I know a couple of bakers who could whip up the perfect tropical wedding cake. I'd be happy to find dresses for you and the girls at the boutique, and Aunt Rikki may know where we could find tuxedos for guys."

"Or the groomsmen could wear matching aloha shirts," Mia chimed in, nodding her head excitedly.

Emma and Dante looked at each other. "What do you think?" Dante asked softly, stroking his bride's cheek.

She squeezed his arm, and her lips stretched wide—it was the first time I'd seen her smile since before we'd found Valentina. "I love it," she said, meeting my gaze. "A destination wedding. Kaley, you're a genius!"

"Sure. Go with *her* idea," Coco muttered bitterly.

I ignored her. "Great," I breathed. Relief flooded through me. "We could even go to the boutique to try on dresses right now, if you like. Jamie's working this morning, and I'm sure she'd be happy to help us." I beamed at the engaged couple. "And when we're done there, I've still got a reservation for us at the resort spa. A little retail therapy followed by some pampering would do us all some good right about now."

"That sounds perfect!" Emma's smile was radiant. She hopped to her feet and threw her arms around me. "Thank you," she whispered, squeezing me tightly.

I caught Coco scowling at me from over Emma's shoulder. I suppressed the urge to stick my tongue out at her. Her gaze lowered to Val's purse, which was still draped over my shoulder along with my tote bag. She flinched, and a wrinkle creased her forehead. I felt a jolt of alarm. *Does she recognize the bag, too?* I stepped away from Emma, subtly pushing the purse behind my back and out of Coco's view.

We said our goodbyes to Dante as he excused himself to join the guys for an afternoon at the pool. Emma took a few moments to freshen her makeup and announced that she was ready to head over to the boutique. As the other girls filed out into the hallway, I paused to search the room for a place to stash Valentina's purse for safekeeping until I heard from Detective Ray. I opened the bottom drawer of the little bedside dresser and shoved it inside. Then I hoisted my tote bag higher on my shoulder and hurried out of the room to join the others.

The Happy Hula Dress Boutique was empty of customers when we arrived a few minutes later. Jamie and one of our sales associates, Rose, were keeping themselves busy by tidying the jewelry display at the front counter. They looked up when we stepped inside, and Rose's brown eyes lit up at the sight of potential customers. She pasted a warm smile on her face and strode toward us, no doubt eager to earn a commission.

"Hi, Kaley," Rose said cheerily, looking from me to the other women. "Can I help your friends find anything in particular?"

I beamed at my pretty, ebony-skinned coworker. "You sure can." I gestured to Emma. "My friend is getting married here on the island, and she needs a dress. The bridesmaids will need something to wear as well," I added, pointing to Coco and Mia. "The three of us."

"And Jamie," Emma piped up. She sent a shy look toward the slender blonde behind the cash register. "If you don't mind stepping in, I mean."

Jamie's blue-green eyes went wide with surprise. "Really?" she asked, her excitement evident in her tone. "I'd love to."

Emma clapped her hands and gave an excited squeal. "Perfect!" she gushed. She turned her attention to Rose. "So, we'll need matching dresses for all four bridesmaids—something tropical, with a floral pattern, maybe. And for me"—she paused, rubbing her chin in thought—"do you have anything in white linen?"

Rose grinned. "I know just the thing," she said, taking Emma by the elbow and guiding her toward a dress rack near the back of the store. Mia and Coco followed.

I hung back and waited for Jamie as she stepped out from behind the counter. "Seems like I missed a lot this morning," she said, lowering her voice so the other girls couldn't hear. "Since when are Emma and Dante tying the knot on the island?"

"Since Detective Ray banned the wedding party from leaving Aloha Lagoon until Val's killer is caught," I replied in the same hushed tone. "Em was crushed that she was going miss her own wedding, so I did the only thing I could think of and suggested that she and Dante hold the ceremony here in Hawaii."

"Good thinking," Jamie said, bumping my fist. "How can I help?"

I thought for moment. "Emma likes the idea of a cliffside wedding, but we still need an officiant, as well as a photographer and someone to bake the cake. Could you contact the Blue Hawaii Chapel and see if Pastor Dan is available for the day after tomorrow? And I'll call Jimmy Toki and see if I can get in touch with his photographer friend, Amy."

"Autumn," Jamie corrected me. "Her name is Autumn Season."

"Whoops." I made a face. "Right, sorry. I'll try to get in touch with her and see if she's free to snap some wedding photos. Then we'll just need to see if Liam Bentley and his grandmother can whip up a cake, and we should be all set. Aside from the dresses, of course." I gestured to the back of the store, where Rose was holding up a pink and green flowery halter dress in front of Mia.

"Sounds like you've got everything worked out," Jamie remarked. "But what about Val's murder? Pick up any new leads?"

"You're not going to believe it," I whispered.

"Ooh." Jamie leaned forward, her expression eager. "Give me the deets."

I shook my head. "Not out here."

She grabbed my arm. "Then let's take this somewhere a little more private." Jamie tugged me toward the back of the store. "Come on, Kaley. Your aunt brought your credit card and spare keys," she said loudly as we passed Emma and the others. "They're in the office."

"Be right back, Em," I called.

Emma didn't respond, too preoccupied with riffling through a rack of linen tunics.

Jamie and I hurried down the hallway that led to the stock room and the little office that I shared with Harmony and Aunt Rikki. I knocked once before opening the door and poking my head inside, relieved to find it empty.

"I think Rikki and Harm are in the stock room unpacking that new shipment of Donna Karan wrap dresses," Jamie said from behind me.

We stepped into the office, and I sank into a chair as Jamie closed the door and then folded herself into the seat facing mine from across the desk. "Your passport, credit card, and spare house key are in the top left drawer," she said. "Rikki told me where she put them in case you dropped in while she was at lunch." She crossed one long leg over the other and leaned forward. "Now, spill. What did you find out?"

"I'm not even sure where to begin," I said, thinking back over the morning's events as I opened the desk drawer and retrieved my belongings. I deposited them in my tote bag and then looked up at Jamie. "Let's see. I guess I'll start with the voice mail I received from Gabby LeClair. Noa brought my new phone over this morning, and I had a message from Gabby that she'd left yesterday." My stomach clenched as I recalled Noa's awkward reaction to my accidental declaration of love—which wasn't an *actual* declaration of love, I swear!—but I forced it to the back of my mind and pressed on. "She said that Koma had found my purse on the party bus and that she was holding it for me in her office."

Jamie frowned. "But your purse—"

"Was found on the beach with Valentina," I finished for her, nodding. "Right. Apparently, Gabby didn't get that memo. When I showed up to claim the bag, she gave me Val's purse, thinking it was mine." I shrugged my shoulders. "I guess neither she nor Koma checked inside the bag to look for an ID since they assumed it belonged to me. It's the same color and style as the purse I'd asked them to look for."

"Wow." Jamie uncrossed her legs and leaned forward in her chair. "Was there anything interesting inside?"

"Interesting is an understatement." I propped my elbows on the desk and leaned forward. "I found a receipt from a drugstore in Atlanta. Val bought a home pregnancy test the day before she arrived on the island."

Jamie's jaw dropped. "Are you for real? She was preggers?" She blew out a low whistle and shook her head, a pained expression stretching across her face. "Holy crap. That's terrible."

I held up a hand. "For all we know the test could have turned out negative," I said. "So it could be nothing." I met her gaze. "But I can't help but wonder, you know? I mean, did you actually see Val drink anything when we were at the club on Thursday night?"

Jamie thought for a moment, her thin brows knitting together. "I don't remember," she said, frowning. "I assumed so at the time, but I wasn't really paying attention to her."

"Same here." I sighed. "Anyway, that's just the first crazy thing that happened this morning. I bumped into Freddy and Will outside the Loco Moco Café earlier, and they invited me to join them on the patio for breakfast. Bryan was there, and I figured that maybe I could get his alibi."

"Do you think he knew about the pregnancy test?" Jamie watched me, unblinking. She was hanging on my every word.

I shrugged. "I didn't get a chance to find out. Tom would barely let me say a word to Bryan—but I *did* find out something else. Bryan and Tom left the table for a minute, and Freddy started telling me about this guy who'd been stalking Valentina back in Atlanta."

"She had a stalker?" Jamie's freckled nose crinkled. "Ew. Creepy."

"No kidding." A little shudder worked its way down my spine. "Freddy said he was the one who told Bryan about the guy. Bryan claimed he would deal with the creeper—but when Freddy asked him about it later, Bryan shut him down. He wouldn't talk about it." I straightened in my seat. "Now, I'm grasping at straws here, but what if Val was romantically involved with this overzealous fan of hers? Or, rather, what if Bryan thought she was?"

"Is Bryan the jealous type?" Jamie asked.

I nodded. "He didn't like it when I so much as looked at other guys—go figure he's the one who wound up cheating on *me*. But he also cares more about his image than the women in his life. If he thought Valentina was being unfaithful and that people knew about it, it would have made him really angry."

"Angry enough to kill her?" Jamie's expression grew troubled.

I shrugged. "I honestly don't know." Another shudder ran through me as I considered that I'd once been married to a man who could turn out to be a murderer.

"But could he have done it if he knew she was pregnant?" Jamie questioned. "It takes a pretty sick person to do something like that."

I swallowed. What if that had been what they were arguing about the night she was killed? If Val had confessed to an affair that led to her pregnancy, could Bryan have been enraged enough to kill her and the baby? "No," I said finally. "Bryan's a jerk, but he's not a monster." If he'd even had an inkling that she might have been pregnant, he wouldn't have hurt her. *But if he didn't know...*

I drew in a breath and blew it out, eager to switch gears. "Then there's Coco," I said, flicking a gaze toward the door. "She was jealous of Valentina, and we already know she followed Val and Bryan at The Lava Pot just before Val was killed."

"So, hypothetically, Coco may have caught up to her out on the beach," Jamie supplied. "Maybe they fought over Bryan and things got out of hand." Her lips parted, and her eyes grew wide. "What if *she* knew about Valentina's baby? That would mean a long-term commitment between Bryan and Val. Think Coco's twisted enough to have offed her squad mate anyway?"

"I don't know." I frowned. "I think for now it's best if we don't mention the pregnancy test to anyone else, though— especially since we don't know for sure if Val was actually pregnant. For now, my next step is to try to find out for sure where Coco went when she left The Lava Pot. I doubt I'll ever be able to get her to open up to me, though."

Jamie's mouth quirked. "Oh, we'll find a way." She hopped up from her chair and beckoned for me to join her. "Come on."

We returned to the sales floor to find that Aunt Rikki and Harmony had emerged from the stock room and had joined the others in front of the changing stalls. Rikki looked up as we approached, her brown eyes twinkling with excitement.

"*Ku'uipo*, you didn't tell me we had the honor of dressing your friend for her wedding."

"It's sort of last minute," I replied, leaning in to give her a hug. "Thanks for bringing my stuff," I added, reaching into my bag to hold up my spare keys and passport. "I'm not sure if I'll ever get my purse back from the police. I should probably cancel all my cards and order replacements."

Rikki squeezed my arm. "If you need money in the meantime, please don't hesitate to ask."

"Your aunt is such a sweetheart," Em called from inside one of the changing room stalls. "She just offered to give me the employee discount on all of our dresses."

"That's so generous of you," Mia added, beaming at Rikki.

"It's my pleasure." My aunt bowed slightly. The sound of a ringing phone filtered down the hall. "Oh! That could be Nani," she said. "I asked her to call me at the shop today so we could schedule my next ukulele lesson. Excuse me." Rikki turned and sprinted toward the office.

"Sheesh," Coco muttered, glancing at the tag on the dress she was holding. "She'd better be giving us a discount— these prices are highway robbery." She met my gaze, sneering. "I always knew you were a crook, Kaley. You probably only married Bryan for his money."

Harmony snorted. "Oh, I like her," she said, smiling wickedly at me. "Finally, someone else who sees through your whole Little Miss Perfect facade." She stepped forward and held out her hand to Coco. "I'm Harmony Kane."

Coco's eyes narrowed skeptically as she sized up the tall, raven-haired woman with her supermodel physique, and I could practically see the jealousy burning behind her expression. After a moment, though, her face relaxed, and she smiled as she took Harmony's hand. "I'm Nicole, but you can call me Coco." She pointed to Harm's soft pink, off-the-shoulder blouse. "I just *love* that top," she gushed. "You've got great taste—unlike some people." She gave my pale blue, ruffle-hemmed shirt a pointed look.

"Great," I mumbled to Jamie. "They're twin terrors."

Jamie nudged me with her elbow. "This might be the in with Coco that we're looking for," she whispered back.

I frowned at her for a second, confused. When Jamie subtly inclined her head toward Harmony, I caught on. "Hey, Harm, your lunch break is coming up soon, right?" I asked, pasting what I hoped was an innocent smile on my face. "Why don't you join us over at the resort spa?"

Harmony's gaze snapped to me. "What's the catch?" she asked, her tone filled with suspicion.

"I booked six mani-pedi appointments for noon," I explained. "We've got room for one more in our group if you'd like to come. It's already paid for." I decided not to mention that the open appointment belonged to a dead woman.

The door to one of the dressing rooms opened, and all heads turned toward Emma as she stepped out in an elegant, sleeveless white linen dress.

"Em, you look gorgeous," I breathed.

The other girls echoed my sentiment, nodding their heads in enthusiastic approval.

Emma beamed at us. "Thanks. I think this is the one!" She turned her attention to Harmony. "Kaley's right—you should come."

"Say yes!" Coco chimed in, not sounding the least bit mournful that Harmony was replacing her fallen cheer mate. She grabbed my coworker's arm. "Come on. It'll be fun."

Harmony glanced my way again. "And I don't have to pay you back?" She still didn't look convinced.

"Nope." *Not with money, anyway.*

Harm squinted at me for a few more seconds. Then she cracked a grin, seemingly satisfied. "In that case, I'd love to. Thanks."

Emma returned to the dressing room to change while Rose ushered Mia and Coco into the other two stalls to try on the dresses that the bride had picked out for them. As soon as Coco was out of earshot, I gripped Harmony by the wrist.

"Hey!" she protested when I pulled her into the hallway, Jamie following behind us.

I held a finger to my lips to warn her to keep quiet. "Okay, look," I said in a low voice. "You don't have to pay anyone back for the trip to the spa, but I do need a favor. A big one."

Harmony scowled. "What kind of favor?" She wrenched her wrist out of my grasp and took a step back. "Favors for you usually lead to trouble."

"No trouble," Jamie said breezily, stepping in front of Harmony. "We just want you to sit next to Coco and chat with her while you're having your nails done." Her lips quirked. "And if you're short on conversation topics, maybe you could try finding out where she was when her friend was killed the other night."

"Oh, I see what's going on here." Harmony looked from Jamie to me and folded her arms across her chest. "You think this chick had something to do with that murder over on the beach. You want me to get her alibi."

Gee, nothing gets past you, Harm. I stifled an eye roll and nodded. "All you have to do is dish with her a little and see if she'll open up to you." I knew Harmony couldn't resist a chance to hear some good gossip.

She studied me for a few seconds, frowning as she weighed her options. "If I help you, what's in it for me?"

"Besides the free mani-pedi?" I bit back a sigh. "How about this? If you can get Coco to tell you her alibi for the time of Valentina's murder, then I'll swap shifts with you and cover mornings at the store for a week, starting next week. *And*," I added, holding up a finger as she began to shake her head, "I'll throw in my green, strapless Dolce & Gabbana dress."

Harmony's perfect brows reached for her hairline. Though she loved to pick apart my wardrobe, I'd caught her admiring the dress the few times I'd worn it at the resort. Harm had an affinity for high-end fashion, but she'd recently fallen on some hard financial times, making it difficult for her to afford the designer threads she adored on her retail salary. "You're serious?" she asked, her tone disbelieving.

"Yep. The dress is yours—but only if you get Coco's alibi."

Pleasure flickered across her face, but she quickly forced it back. Harmony lifted her chin. "Well, your dress will definitely be too big for *me*, but I suppose I can pair it with a belt to cinch the waist." She nodded. "Okay. You've got a deal. I'll just go let Rikki know that I'm taking my lunch break now." She stepped into the office and closed the door behind her.

"Is she for real?" Jamie scoffed, looking me up and down. "Why on earth would she think a dress of yours would be too big for her?"

I glanced down at my size four waist and rolled my eyes. "Let her get her digs in. At least she agreed to help." I met her gaze. "That was a great idea, by the way. Harmony and Coco are kindred, rotten spirits. If she'll spill her alibi to anyone, Harm's probably our best bet."

Jamie bumped my fist. "I've got your back. I just can't believe you agreed to give her that Dolce & Gabbana dress." She shook her head. "It must have cost a fortune."

I grinned. "It's a knockoff."

Jamie's eyes widened a fraction. Then she smirked. "Well, that's a twist I didn't see coming."

I winked at her and held up a finger to my lips. "Our little secret."

CHAPTER ELEVEN

———

Jamie hurried toward the front counter to assist a customer who'd wandered in as Coco and Mia walked out of their changing stalls, wearing twin pink and teal floral dresses. Rose thrust a matching garment into my hands. "The bride wants to see how you all look in these before she makes a decision. I have one in Jamie's size as well, whenever she gets a chance to come try it on."

Emma emerged from her own dressing room, back in her robin's egg blue capris and frilly white top. I took her place in the stall and quickly slipped out of my clothes and into the dress she'd picked out for me.

"Kaley, you look adorable!" Em cooed when I stepped out to model the outfit. "I think these will be perfect."

Tonya, our afternoon cashier, arrived to relieve Jamie for her lunch break just in time for her to try on her own bridesmaid garb. When we'd all changed back into our normal clothes, Emma grabbed her credit card and walked up to the front counter to have Tonya ring up the outfits. Rose followed and tried to up-sell her with some necklaces and bracelets.

Harmony rejoined our group as we headed for the front door. "All ready," she said. "Rikki's giving both Jamie and me an extended lunch hour. She wants us to enjoy ourselves."

"Awesome," Jamie exclaimed.

Harmony made a face. "She thinks it's great that we're bonding," she told me dryly.

I choked back a laugh. *Bonding? With Harmony? Yeah, right.* If it made Rikki happy, I'd let her think what she wanted. "Come on," I said, motioning for the women to exit the store as

Emma grabbed her purchases. "Our appointment is in five minutes."

Emma excused herself to run back to the room and drop off the dresses while the rest of the girls followed me to the Aloha Lagoon Spa, which was located down the hall from the lobby and across from the employee locker room. Chanel, a French-Canadian woman with cherry red hair, checked us in at the front counter before allowing us to browse a collection of nail polish bottles. Once everyone had selected their color of choice, we were seated in a long row of chairs and each served a glass of champagne.

For the next half hour, I sat between Emma and Jamie and indulged in a good old-fashioned pampering session, complete with a foot soak, massage, and a fresh coat of Cerulean Daydream on my fingers and toes. I turned my mind off and lost myself in blissful relaxation while the manicurist worked away on my piggies. I gradually became aware of the conversations around me as the woman began applying a clear top coat over my toe polish.

To my left, Emma hummed to herself as she browsed a magazine. Mia was chatting with Jamie from two seats over on my right. "This is heaven," she said dreamily. "That was the best foot massage I've had in my entire life. I might have to come back here again before we leave."

"You're in good hands with Marta," Jamie agreed, nodding at the spa employee who was painting Mia's toes. The woman smiled bashfully up at them.

"I was so sorry to hear about your friend, Coco." Harmony's voice cut through the idle chatter, and my ears perked up. I glanced past Emma to the two chairs at the end of the row where Harm and Coco were seated. It sounded as if Harmony was keeping up her end of our bargain. "What was the poor girl's name?" she asked, her voice filled with sympathy. "Valencia?"

"Valen*tina*," Coco corrected. She glanced down at the manicurist kneeling at her feet. "Can you add one more coat to my big toe? The color looks a little uneven."

One of the resort employees came over to refill their champagne flutes. Harmony pursed her lips and flicked a glance my way. I nodded encouragingly. She sucked in a breath and shifted her focus back to Coco. "Were you two very close?" She casually sipped her drink.

Coco had already drained half her glass. She gave a dismissive wave. "We cheered together, but I wouldn't say we were the best of friends. Val was too competitive. She had to have everything and everyone she wanted." Coco dropped her gaze, and even from my seat a few chairs away, I could make out the jealous look on her face.

"Oh, I know a girl like that here, too," Harmony said breezily. She cut another look my way. "She thinks she's so hot just because she somehow managed to trick one of the sexiest guys at the resort into going out with her. I don't know what he sees in her—especially when there are much more attractive women on the island."

I ignored the barb. It was no secret that ever since Noa had returned to the islands looking like sex on a surfboard, Harmony had set her sights on him—so she wasn't exactly thrilled when he and I started seeing each other. If she had to gain Coco's trust at my expense, then so be it. Finally finding out whether or not the cheerleader was a coldblooded killer would be worth it.

"It sounds like maybe Val moved in on your man?" There was a question in Harmony's tone.

Coco finished her glass of champagne and gave a tiny hiccup. "Something like that, although the other night, I—" Her words cut off as she seemed to catch herself. "I think this stuff is going to my head," she said with a nervous giggle.

"Relax," Harmony said. "You're on vacation, girl. It's okay to unwind a little." She held out her own glass. "You want some more?"

"Thanks." Coco took the glass and held it to her lips, sipping more slowly this time. "I *do* deserve to let loose, don't I?"

Harmony's plan seemed to be working. *Damn, she's good,* I thought, impressed by her tactics. I leaned slightly forward in my chair, eager to hear what Coco would say next.

"You're all done!" the young woman at my feet chirped, and I nearly jumped. She rose and handed me a pair of foam flip-flops. "Put these on so you don't ruin your nails. Let's get you set up under one of the heat lamps so the polish will dry faster."

I tried to hide my disappointment as I was ushered into another room before I could hear the rest of Coco's conversation with Harmony. Emma was brought into the room a few moments after I sat down. "What do you think of my wedding nails?" Em asked, holding out her fingers to show off the gorgeous opalescent white polish. Her ring finger on each hand was painted the color of the ocean. "That's my 'something blue,'" she said, grinning.

"I love it," I gushed.

Emma's eyes grew misty. "You really saved the day, Kaley. My wedding would be ruined without you."

"You'd have done the same for me," I replied, squeezing her shoulder. I stared at her for a few moments as she settled into her chair and placed her hands and feet under the lamps. On a hunch, I asked, "Hey, Em—you didn't happen to notice anything off about Val on Thursday night, did you?"

Her brow furrowed, and she turned her head so that she was facing me. "What do you mean?"

I shrugged. "There's just something that's been bothering me. At the club, did you happen to notice how much Valentina had to drink?" *If she even drank at all,* I added silently. "Did she take the shot you bought her when we first got there?"

Emma frowned. "I don't know," she said slowly, giving me a confused look. "I think so. Val wasn't one to turn down free booze."

"Were you two close?" I asked. "I mean, after I moved away, did you become better friends with her?"

Emma made a face. "Well, she *was* dating my fiancé's best friend," she said, her tone guilty. "So we saw a lot of each other. I don't want you to think I was betraying you by being nice to her," she added with a sigh. "But Val did have her moments. She could be a good person when she wanted to be."

I pushed back the pang of jealousy. Emma and I used to be close, but ever since she'd arrived on the island, it felt like there was a rift between us. I'd only been gone from Atlanta for a short while, but it seemed that was long enough for us to have drifted apart.

"I'm not mad at you," I said softly. "I just wondered if you and Val had a good relationship. One where she might open up to you about a secret if she were keeping one."

"What kind of secret?" Emma's frown deepened. "Something she was keeping from Bryan?"

"Possibly," I replied, picturing the receipt with the pregnancy test on it. I didn't want to come clean about what I knew and risk Emma having another prewedding meltdown. She was under a lot of stress, and the idea that her dead friend could have had a bun in the oven would be more than enough to push her over the edge. "I'm just trying to get to the bottom of why someone would have wanted her dead," I said.

A dark cloud settled over Emma's features. "Kaley, you're not trying to find the killer yourself, are you? That sounds dangerous."

I opened my mouth to respond but closed it as Mia and Jamie entered the room. "So, what should we do next?" Mia asked as she sat down and placed her nails under the heat lamp.

"Well, the nail work is already paid for, but for a small up-charge, you can pay to add a deep-tissue massage," Jamie told her. "I usually go for that myself. Afterward, I like to relax in the sauna for a few minutes."

I pulled my nails away from the lamp and checked to be sure they were dry. "That sounds like a great idea," I said, rising from my seat. "I think I'll skip the massage and head straight for the sauna. Emma, want to join me?" I asked, hoping we could continue our conversation in private.

"Actually, I think I'll get that massage," she said, avoiding my gaze. "It's part of the package you gave me, and it sounds like just the thing I need to relax right now. Maybe we can meet up outside at the pool after? I'd love to get a little sun before the luau tonight. Speaking of"—she fixed me with a hopeful expression—"is there any chance you could get some extra tickets for the guys? I was hoping they could join us."

"I'll see what I can do," I said, trying to hide my disappointment. I couldn't shake the feeling that Emma was avoiding being alone with me. In fact, it felt as if she'd been doing just that ever since we'd found Val's body on the beach. *But why?*

"A massage sounds good to me, too." Mia nodded. "Tell them to book me a table, too, and I'll join you as soon as my nails are dry."

I watched as Emma hopped out of her seat and walked over to the spa's reception desk. Then I slipped my tote bag over my shoulder and said goodbye to the others before heading for the employee locker room. Once I was around the corner, I retrieved my phone from my bag and fired off a text to Harmony, asking her to meet me in the sauna so she could fill me in on what she'd learned from Coco. Then I shrugged out of my clothes and grabbed an oversized white towel from a basket near the door. Wrapping the towel securely around my body, I stowed my clothes in a free locker and padded barefoot toward the sauna.

I opened the door and stepped inside, letting the heat roll over me. The dimly lit room wasn't much larger than a walk-in closet, with cedar benches lining three of the walls. A trough full of hot stones rested against the fourth. I perched in the corner of the empty room and leaned back, closing my eyes and letting the warmth melt the tension from my body.

A few minutes later, I heard the door open. I cracked open an eyelid as Harmony stepped inside. She'd piled her black hair high in a messy bun and had also wrapped herself in one of the large, white towels.

"Good, you got my text," I said, sitting up straight.

Harmony dropped onto a bench on the opposite end of the room. She scowled at me. "I wanted to get a massage," she pouted.

"We'll make this quick." I leaned forward, meeting her gaze. "Did you get anything out of Coco?"

Harmony crossed one leg over the other and settled back against the wall. She closed her eyes. "Not really. I thought I could get her gabbing if she was tipsy, but no such luck. All I know is that she went to The Lava Pot just before it closed and then decided to go for a walk down by the beach." She opened her eyes and looked at me. "She did say that she saw your ex-hubby and his girlfriend at the bar, though."

"I already knew about that," I said, unable to hide the frustration from my tone. "Did she happen to mention why she didn't approach them at The Lava Pot? The bartender told me she just sat at the bar and watched them from across the room."

Harmony shrugged. "I don't know. She did say that they seemed to be arguing about something, but that's all I got out of her before our nails were done." She folded her arms over her chest. "I kept my end of the deal, though," she said with a greedy smile. "So you can bring my dress to the shop sometime next week when you cover my morning shifts."

I wiped the sweat from my brow. "Sure," I said absently, shifting my attention to the box of steaming rocks along the opposite wall. I squinted. Was it my imagination, or were they burning a little brighter than usual? Several more beads of sweat rolled down my face, and I rubbed them away with the back of my hand before drying it off on my towel. I swallowed, realizing I was suddenly parched. It definitely felt like the temperature had ratcheted up several degrees since I'd entered the sauna.

"I think I've reached my limit," I said, climbing off of the wooden bench.

"Me too," Harmony agreed. I could see the sheen of perspiration on her face and neck. "I need to hit the water cooler."

I placed a hand on the door and pushed. It didn't budge. Frowning, I pushed harder. Still nothing. "Does this thing always stick?" I asked Harmony as I tried again.

"No." She snorted. "Maybe you're just out of shape."

I rolled my eyes. Sure, I wasn't exactly Superwoman, but I also wasn't lacking in the arm-strength department, thanks to Aunt Rikki insisting that I tag along to her sunrise yoga classes over the past few weeks. I gave the door another shove, this time leaning my shoulder into it. "I think it's really stuck," I said. Despite the extreme heat, I could feel the hairs on the back of my neck stand on end.

Harmony heaved an exasperated sigh. "Do I have to do everything?" she groused. She eyed me impatiently. "At least move over so I can give it a try."

I stepped out of her way, and she held up her towel with one hand while pressing the door firmly with the other. Her irritated look melted away, and her brows lifted in confusion. "What the..." Harm's voice trailed off as she pushed the door again. She secured her towel more tightly around her and then placed both hands on the door. Her body tensed, and the tendons in her neck strained as she shoved. "Why won't this freaking thing open?" she asked through clenched teeth.

I joined her, and together we threw our full body weight against the door, but it was no use. Panic seized my chest, and I looked up to find the same emotion reflected in Harmony's wide eyes. "Let's try to be calm," I said, though my voice shook. "Jamie was going to come join me in the sauna after her massage. She should be here any minute. Maybe she can open the door from the other side."

"Or maybe we can yell loud enough to get the attention of the spa staff," Harmony suggested. I could hear a nervous tremble in her voice. She began to bang her fists against the door. "Help!" she cried. "We can't get the door open!" She paused, and we waited a few beats, listening for a response. There was none. Harmony began to pant. "Does it feel like it's getting hotter in here to you?" she gasped, wiping more beads of sweat from her face.

I nodded. "It could just be that we're exerting so much energy trying to get the door open," I said, though the visceral tug in my middle section made me think otherwise.

Harm tapped at the little black strap on her wrist and then shook her head. "No." Now her voice was high with unmistakable panic. "According to the thermometer on my fitness band, it's jumped seven degrees since I first came in here." She gulped. "Make that nine. It's getting hotter—and fast."

"Do you think the door could have locked by accident?" I asked, still struggling not to let the panic take over.

Harmony's breathing became ragged, and she flung herself at the door again. "I can't die in here," she wailed, pummeling the wood with both hands. "Somebody please help!"

I finally abandoned my own sense of composure and joined in, screaming and pounding my fists against the door. The heat was suffocating, and I gasped for air in between cries for help. It was getting harder to breathe. *We really could die in here*, I thought, frantically clawing at the sauna door.

Together, Harmony and I launched ourselves at the door once more in a desperate attempt to break it down. Just as we slammed into the wood, it gave way, swinging quickly outward. We toppled into the spa's immaculate hallway, landing in a pile of towels and sweaty limbs. Cool air rolled over me, and I gulped in several mouthfuls of it.

"Holy crap! Are you okay?" Jamie's voice was frantic. "Kaley?" She leaned over me, the color draining from her face. Her blue-green eyes were wide and fearful. "Please be okay. Say something."

"Water," I rasped, struggling to haul myself off of Harmony.

Jamie dashed the few feet down the hall to the water cooler and quickly filled two cups. I smiled weakly when she returned and handed me one. The chilled liquid felt like pure bliss as it slid down my throat.

"Thanks." Still feeling dazed. I glanced at the door to the sauna, which had swung back toward the frame but remained open just a crack. "It was stuck," I told Jamie. "We couldn't push it open."

Jamie's mouth set in a grim line. "Honey, the door wasn't stuck," she said, gesturing behind me.

I followed her gaze, my head swimming with confusion as I stared at one of the large lobby chairs, which was toppled over on its side just beyond the doorway to the sauna. A chill zipped down my spine as the realization sunk in.

As if to confirm my suspicion, Jamie walked over to the chair. Shutting the sauna door, she pushed the fallen piece of furniture against it. On its side, the chair was just wide enough to wedge between the door and the wall of the narrow hallway, preventing the door from budging. "This is how I found it," she said, her voice shaking. She gestured to the thermostat dial on the wall beside the door. "And this was turned all the way up. I think someone trapped you in the sauna on purpose."

CHAPTER TWELVE

"Okay, that is *it*," Harmony said sharply. Her voice was hoarse from screaming. "I'm through doing you favors, Kaley. Every time I try to help you, I almost get killed."

I couldn't argue with her. Harmony had stuck her neck out for me once before, and we'd been lucky to escape with our lives. I struggled to my feet as Jamie moved past me to help Harm stand up. Walking on wobbly legs, I made my way over to the fallen chair.

Someone wanted me to be trapped in the sauna, I thought, staring down at the chair. *And they turned up the heat.* Somebody had been trying to scare me...or maybe even worse. *But who?* My eyes narrowed as I glanced toward the door at the end of the hall, the one that led out to the courtyard swimming pool. I could see a familiar busty blonde standing just outside. *Coco.* Perhaps she'd caught on when Harmony had begun prying for her alibi. Could she have been trying to silence us both?

Not caring that I was still wearing nothing but an oversized towel, I abandoned Jamie and Harm and marched toward the exit. I flung it open, nearly knocking Coco out of the way in the process.

"Hey! Watch it," she cried, staggering backward. She cringed as she took in my blotchy red skin and angry expression. "Yikes. You look even more terrible than usual."

Freddy Jenkins, who'd been standing beside Coco, also flinched. "What happened, Kaley?" he asked. "Are you all right?"

I shook my head. "*You*," I hissed, pointing a finger at Coco. I opened my mouth, prepared to tear into her, when a sudden movement caught my eye. I shifted my focus past Coco and Freddy and felt my blood chill. A man was watching our exchange intently, his thin lips stretched in a look of eager fascination. I recognized his chubby face and beady green eyes. I'd bumped into him earlier as I was leaving the Loco Moco Café. The man's grin evaporated as we locked gazes, and he abruptly turned and began walking briskly across the patio.

I gripped my towel tightly and pushed past Coco and Freddy. "Hey," I called out, waving my free hand at the man. "Wait!" I lurched after him but only made it a few feet. Being overheated had zapped most of my strength. A wave of dizziness swept over me, and my legs buckled beneath me. I sat down hard on the nearest lounger, watching helplessly as the strange man exited the pool area and melted into the crowd milling about the courtyard.

Freddy was at my side within seconds, with Jamie on his heels. He crouched beside me, his dark eyes full of concern as they searched my face. "What's going on? Do you need me to call the lifeguard over?" He lifted his hand to signal to the bronze-skinned young man sitting atop the lookout chair, but I gripped his arm. "There was this creepy guy," I said hoarsely, pointing toward the courtyard. "In an orange bathing suit and blue Atlanta Braves cap. He—"

"Did he hurt you?" Freddy's face darkened. Without waiting for me to respond, he turned and loped in the direction I'd pointed, his long dreadlocks flying behind him.

Jamie knelt beside me in the space where Freddy had just been. "I saw him too," she said quietly. "Kales, I recognize that guy. He was at the Lanai Lounge the other night."

I blinked at her, feeling cold all over. "He was?"

She nodded, a look of grim certainty on her tanned face. "Yep. He was sitting at the far corner of the bar the whole night. I caught him staring at us a few times, but at the time I didn't think anything of it. I figured maybe he was trying to work up the nerve to hit on one of the girls, but now..." She shuddered. "It just seems like too much of a coincidence that he was here right after someone trapped you in the sauna, right? And the way he just took off running when you spotted him—that was a guilty reaction if I've ever seen one." She grimaced. "Do you think he could be connected to Val's murder somehow?"

I nodded, picturing the man's probing eyes staring at me from underneath that baseball cap. *An Atlanta Braves cap.* That couldn't have been a coincidence, either. I had a sneaking suspicion I knew exactly who the man was. "Remember how I mentioned that Valentina had a stalker?"

Jamie's eyes went wide. "You think that was him? That he followed her all the way to Hawaii?"

I nodded grimly. "Of course, I don't know for sure. Freddy didn't seem to have noticed him before I came outside, but if he manages to catch up to the creep then maybe he can identify him. He's seen the stalker before, following Val through the parking lot at the football stadium." A sudden shudder worked its way through me, and I wrapped my arms tightly around my middle. Though I wanted to join Freddy in chasing after the alleged stalker, I was too exhausted and dehydrated.

Jamie must have seen my distress in my face. "Come on," she said, offering me her hand. "My lunch break is up. I've got to get back to the shop, but first, let's get your clothes and a big glass of water."

I allowed her to help me up from the lounger, and together we made our way back toward the door to the spa. We'd only gone a few feet when a small, dark square on the patio tiles caught my eye. I halted and stooped for closer inspection. It was a brown leather wallet with the initials *A.R.* engraved in the top corner.

"I should take this over to the pool bar," I said, picking it up and flipping it open. "I'm sure they have a lost and found—" I stopped talking as my gaze landed on the driver's license inside. Staring up at me from the little plastic card was the face of the man who'd just fled the pool area. I glanced at the name and Georgia address on the ID and felt a smile curve over my lips. Had I just stumbled upon the identity of Valentina's stalker?

"On second thought," I said, holding up the license so that Jamie could see. "I think I'll hold on to it for now. I'd like to return it in person so I can have a word with Mr. Andrew Ryan from Atlanta."

Jamie bumped my fist. "Brilliant! Just promise me one thing," she said, her grin fading slightly. "Wait until I get off work to go looking for him, okay? Right now you need some rest, and Noa would kill me if I let you go after some creeper dude alone."

I bit back a sigh. She'd made two good points. "Deal," I said reluctantly. "But as soon as your shift is over, we're going to track down this Andrew jerk. I need some answers."

* * *

Freddy returned to the pool area empty-handed after a few minutes of pursuit. He'd been unable to find the fleeing Mr. Ryan. Mia and Emma escorted me back to the room and left me there alone, insisting I get some rest, though I didn't manage to sleep a wink. Instead, I lay on the bed, staring at Andrew Ryan's wallet. I went through its contents several times, but nothing stood out as suspicious; it only contained a driver's license, one bank card, one credit card, and a handful of small bills. I was disappointed that there wasn't a room key inside. Without one, I couldn't be sure whether he was actually staying at the resort or if he had booked lodging nearby and had sneaked onto the property to spy on us.

But why? I wondered as I turned the wallet over in my hands. If he really was Valentina's stalker, what reason would he have to stick around and watch our group now that she was dead? Had he set his sights on a new woman to harass, or could he be trying to ensure that no one had connected him to the crime?

A shiver worked its way through me as I recalled bumping into the man in the café that morning, less than an hour after I'd tracked down Val's purse. I was starting to suspect that the seemingly innocent encounter had been more than a mere coincidence. Then there was the fact that he'd been at the pool, just a few yards away from the spa, when Harmony and I had been trapped and nearly cooked to death in the sauna. It was entirely possible that he could have slipped inside and wedged that chair between the door and the wall to block our escape. Had he been following me all day, waiting for a chance to attack?

After two hours, Jamie knocked on the door of our room. Though she was an hour earlier than expected, having convinced

Aunt Rikki to let her leave work ahead of schedule, I was already dressed and ready to go look for Andrew Ryan. I shared my suspicions with her as we made our way to the main lobby.

"And a new name enters the suspect pool," she said wearily. "That makes three people who potentially wanted Valentina dead." Her brow furrowed. "It does seem awfully suspicious that this Ryan guy was just outside the spa right after you were trapped," she agreed, frowning. "But if there wasn't a room key in his wallet, how are we going to track him down?"

"Just follow my lead," I told her, crossing the crowded lobby toward the front desk. I was relieved to see that Summer wasn't working that afternoon. I didn't want her to think I was making a habit of asking for guests' room numbers. In her place sat a plump girl with a childlike face framed by bushy black hair. "Hi," I said warmly, smiling at her. I glanced at her name tag. "I don't believe I've seen you here before, Kara. Are you new?"

The girl gave me a timid smile. "It's my second day. Summer's been training me, but I'm on my own this afternoon."

Perfect. I felt my smile widen. "Cool. Welcome to the resort." I held out my hand. "I'm Kaley, and this is Jamie. We work at the Happy Hula Dress Boutique out in the courtyard." I glanced at the computer. "Has Summer taught you how to look up a guest's room number yet?" I asked, my tone polite. "We're trying to find a friend of ours who's visiting from the mainland. Would you mind looking up the room number for an Andrew Ryan?"

Kara's forehead wrinkled. "I don't think I'm supposed to give out that kind of information," she said, glancing nervously around the lobby as if looking for someone to back her up.

"Don't worry. It's fine," I assured her. I held up the man's wallet. "We just had lunch with Andy at the Loco Moco a little while ago," I lied, hiking my thumb over my shoulder toward the café entrance. "He left his wallet at the table. I tried calling, but his phone is turned off. We were just hoping to run it up to him. I'd hate for him to think it's been lost or stolen."

"Typical Andy," Jamie chimed in, chuckling. "He'd lose his head if it wasn't screwed on." She smiled pleasantly at the young woman.

Kara chewed her lip, glancing from Jamie to me. Finally, she placed her hands on the keyboard in front of her. "What did you say his last name was?" she asked.

"Ryan," Jamie piped up, grinning at me when the young woman wasn't looking. "Andrew Ryan."

The girl's fingers clacked over a few keys, and then she scanned the screen. "Mr. Ryan is staying in room 313." She pointed across the lobby to the elevators. "Head up to the third floor and take a left."

"Thank you so much, Kara. You're the best."

"Yeah. I'm sure Andy will appreciate it," Jamie added.

I gave the girl one last smile before motioning for Jamie to follow me to the elevators. We made our way up to the third floor, stopping short just a few rooms down from where Andrew Ryan was staying. His door was open, and a housekeeping cart was sticking halfway out into the hall. The sound of a vacuum could be heard coming from inside.

My shoulders slumped. "Just our luck," I muttered to Jamie. "I guess we'll have to come back later. At least we know his room number now." I started to turn back toward the elevators, but Jamie grabbed my arm.

"Are you kidding?" she asked, her voice low. There was a glint of mischief in her aquamarine eyes. "It's actually a good thing he's not in there right now. That means we have time to do a little snooping before we talk to him. We can check for anything suspicious."

"Like what?" I asked. "A murder weapon?"

She shrugged. "Who knows what we might find?"

I frowned. "I don't think that housekeeping is going to take too kindly to us barging in and digging through his stuff."

She winked. "The maid won't even know what's happening. I've got a plan." Jamie filled me in on her idea, which I had to admit wasn't too shabby. When the whirring sound of the vacuum ceased a few moments later, I moved quickly past the door to room 313 and leaned against the wall just outside it, waiting. The supply cart rolled out into the hall, followed by a middle-aged Polynesian woman with graying hair. Before she could glance in my direction, Jamie walked up to her from the other end of the hall, waving to get her attention.

"Excuse me, ma'am," she said, coming to a stop next to the cart filled with shampoo, conditioner, and other toiletries. She made a show of rolling her eyes. "My boyfriend used all the conditioner, and I need to wash this ratty mop of mine." She gestured to her short blonde hair, which looked anything but ratty. "Could I trouble you for a few more bottles?"

I didn't wait to hear the woman's response. While the housekeeper's back was turned, I slipped through the open door into Andrew Ryan's room, quickly ducking around the corner. Seconds later, the door clicked shut. I tiptoed back over to it and leaned forward, listening to Jamie's muffled words on the other side. Her voice moved farther away as she walked down the hall with the woman. When I was sure that I was alone, I turned and surveyed my surroundings.

The curtains were pulled back, letting natural light illuminate the room. The housekeeper had made the bed and had placed fresh towels on the corner of the comforter, along with a couple of mints wrapped in green aluminum foil. A pile of rumpled clothes sat on the bedside table. I figured the woman had probably picked them up off the floor so she could vacuum.

I cautiously moved through the room, staying as silent as possible so I could hear if anyone approached from outside in the hall. Andrew's black vinyl suitcase was on the desk. I unzipped it and opened each flap and pocket, unsure exactly what I was looking for. *A bludgeoning weapon of some sort? A lock of Valentina's hair? A signed confession?* Instead, all I found were several pairs of swim trunks, some white undershirts, a bottle of suntan lotion, and an old Dean Koontz novel. Nothing that screamed *I'm a psycho stalker.*

I dropped down to my knees and peeked under the bed, but nothing was there, either. A cursory search of the bathroom also proved fruitless. I was on the brink of giving up and heading back into the hallway when my phone began to buzz. Jamie's name flashed across the screen.

"This search is a bust," I said as soon as I placed the phone to my ear. "There's nothing in—"

"Get out now!" she exclaimed in a shrill whisper. "I'm downstairs in the lobby, and Andrew just got on an elevator. He had his room key in his hand. I think he's headed your way."

Adrenaline zipped through me. "Thanks," I whispered back. "I'll meet you downstairs." I scrambled out of the bathroom and started for the door that led back into the hall. Just as I reached for the handle, I heard footsteps approaching. A man cleared his throat, and the scratching sound of the plastic room key card touching the wood sent my pulse into overdrive. I jerked back around, searching frantically for a place to hide. The closet door was several feet away. The little key card sensor beeped as I lunged for the closet and slipped inside, pulling the door closed as quietly as I could. A fraction of a second later, I heard Andrew Ryan step into the room.

I was trapped.

CHAPTER THIRTEEN

———

Andrew whistled the theme from *Hawaii Five-0* as he ambled into the room, walking slowly past my hiding place. My heart was pounding so loudly in my ears that I was pretty sure it could be heard all the way from the elevators. I held my breath until I thought my lungs would burst, waiting for the man who might have murdered Valentina Cruz to fling the closet door open and discover me.

Instead, the mattress springs squeaked, and I heard twin thuds as two objects hit the floor. I pictured the man resting his portly frame onto the bed and kicking off his shoes. It sounded as if he was settling in for a while. I could be trapped in this closet for hours, assuming he didn't eventually find me.

Still holding my breath, I was beginning to see stars when I heard the television turn on. My exhale and subsequent gasp for more oxygen were drowned out by the sounds of a game show theme song. At least, I hoped they were. I waited for my breathing to return to normal and then sent a text to Jamie.

I'm hiding in the closet. I don't think I can sneak out without him noticing.

Since it seemed I wasn't going anywhere in the near future, I turned on the flashlight app on my phone to get a better look at my surroundings. A shabby gray sport coat hung from one of the hangers, alongside a pair of equally rumpled pants and a white dress shirt with a coffee stain down the front. A pair of men's dress shoes and two pairs of flip-flops lay at my feet. Just below the pull-down ironing board, I noticed a black leather briefcase.

I carefully sank into a seated position on the closet floor, pulling my knees close to my chest to fit in the cramped space.

As quietly as I could, I reached for the briefcase, slowly undoing the outside clasp. Inside the case were a small laptop and several manila file folders.

I pulled out the first folder and flipped it open, feeling the hairs prickle on the back of my neck. It contained a stack of printed photos, all of which featured Valentina. There were pictures of the young woman climbing into her car in a dark parking deck and some of her walking through what I recognized as Phipps Plaza in Buckhead, her arms laden with shopping bags. There were even a few photos of Val with Bryan. Their backs were facing the camera as they walked toward the ground floor entrance to the building that housed the condo I'd previously shared with my ex-hubby.

Busted, I thought, flipping through the rest of the folder and taking in the dozens of photos the creepy man had snapped. Freddy had been right. Andrew Ryan had definitely been stalking Valentina.

My phone vibrated in my hand, causing me to jump. It slipped from my fingers and landed on the floor beside me with a hard thud. Outside the closet, the TV clicked off. My heart leapt to my throat as the mattress creaked again. I heard Andrew's feet hit the floor and begin padding closer to my hiding spot. It looked like I was about to be busted, too.

I nearly wilted with relief when, at the last moment, the man's footsteps veered in the direction of the bathroom. The door closed behind him, and after a few moments, the sound of running water reached my ears. He was taking a shower. *Now's my chance,* I thought, scooping up my fallen phone. I started to slip the folders containing the man's pictures of Valentina back into the bag but hesitated. Pulling up my phone's camera, I snapped a few photos of my own, making copies of his images that I could show Detective Ray. Though I was pretty sure I'd wind up in hot water if I stole the evidence, maybe showing him my digital copies of the pics would be enough to convince him to redirect his investigation toward Andrew Ryan.

I dropped my phone back into my pocket and returned the folder to the briefcase. Then I opened the closet door just a crack. I cautiously poked my head out to make absolutely sure the coast was clear. The afternoon sunlight spilled into the empty room, and the sound of the running shower filtered out from the bathroom. I climbed out of the closet and dashed toward the door, flinging it open. As I burst into the hallway, I collided with a wall of solid muscle. I skittered back a step and gaped up into the face of a very panicked-looking Noa.

"Are you all right?" he demanded, pulling me out of the doorway. He frantically looked me over. "Did he try to hurt you? Where is he?" He shot a glance over my shoulder toward Andrew's room, his eyes blazing.

I eased out of Noa's grasp. "I'm fine. And no, he didn't hurt me—he never even saw me. I was hiding in the closet." I dropped my gaze to the carpet, feeling sheepish. When I looked up again, his expression had darkened.

"What were you thinking, Kales?" His jaw clenched. "What if you'd been caught?"

My face felt hot. "What are you even doing here? And how did you know where I was?" I asked, though I had a feeling I already knew the answer. My suspicion was confirmed a moment later when the elevator dinged at the end of the hall. The double doors opened, and Jamie emerged. She took one look at Noa and me, and her expression turned guilty. She did an about-face and marched right back into the elevator, shooting me an apologetic look as the doors closed again.

Thanks a lot, I thought darkly.

"I brought my laptop over to the Loco Moco to get some work done out on the patio," Noa said, his expression still hard. "And it's a good thing I did, considering your knack for getting into trouble."

"Look, I'm sorry," I said, grabbing his arm and pulling him down the hall, putting distance between us and the stalker's room. "Just save the lecture for after we get out of here."

Thankfully, Noa didn't argue. He let me lead him toward the elevators, and we waited in sulky silence until the one Jamie had just taken downstairs returned to our floor. When the doors reopened, we stepped inside to join a middle-aged couple. They climbed off on the second floor, and as soon as the doors closed again, Noa rounded on me. His face was tight with anger.

"You should have told me what you were doing," he said. "I shouldn't have to find out from Jamie that you're trapped in an alleged murderer's hotel room." His expression twisted to a look of pain. "If you got hurt, Kaley, I don't know what I would do."

My own anger bubbled to the surface. "Oh, so *now* you care," I snapped, feeling my frustration boil over.

Noa looked as if I'd slapped him. "What is that supposed to mean?" he asked, his voice sounding hurt. "What have I ever done to make you think I don't care about you?"

"It's obvious that you don't want to go to Atlanta and be my date to Emma's wedding," I said sourly. "Though, you'll probably be happy to know that you were right about the police not letting us leave the island—Detective Ray is holding the wedding party here until Valentina's killer is caught. Emma and Dante have decided to get married right here on the island since they're going to miss their ceremony in Georgia, but you know what?" I placed my hands on my hips. "I think I'll just go stag."

Noa opened his mouth to speak, but I didn't wait to hear his response. The elevator stopped on the first floor, and the doors opened, filling the small space with the sounds of the busy lobby. Tears stinging my eyes, I turned away from Noa and marched off.

"Kaley, wait," he called, but I pushed my way through the crowd of guests, putting distance between us.

I walked briskly toward the women's restroom at the edge of the lobby and ducked inside. Guilt soured my stomach as soon as I closed the door behind me. *I shouldn't have snapped at him like that,* I thought, unable to look my reflection in the eye as I leaned against the counter. I grabbed a paper towel from the dispenser and dabbed at my eyes. Noa was right—I shouldn't have put myself in a potentially dangerous situation without telling him. If our roles had been reversed, I'd have been just as furious with him as he was with me now.

It's because he cares about me, I scolded myself. I thought back to his strange reluctance when I'd first invited him to be my date to Emma's wedding. I'd gone from worrying that he was thinking we were moving too fast to suddenly pushing him away. *Real smooth, Kaley.* I swallowed the lump in my throat. I owed Noa an apology and an explanation for my beyond crummy behavior.

I took a deep breath and slowly exhaled, doing my best to compose myself. Then I stepped back out into the hall to find Noa. I retraced my steps and scanned the large atrium but couldn't spot him among the crowd. Sighing, I pulled out my phone and dialed his number, making my way to the courtyard to search for him there. My heart sank as my call was sent straight to voice mail. "Noa, it's Kaley," I said, hearing the quiver in my voice. "Listen, I screwed up. I'm sorry." I hesitated for a moment, feeling more emotional words gather behind my teeth. I stuffed them back down. "Please just call me," I said finally before hanging up.

Shoulders slumped, I shuffled back inside, heading in the direction of my room. Hope bloomed in my chest as my phone began to ring. I pressed it to my ear without even looking at the Caller ID. "Noa, I'm so glad you called me back," I said breathlessly.

"Hello, Ms. Kalua." Detective Ray's voice filled my ear. "I received your message. You said you found something that might aid in my investigation into the murder of Miss Cruz?" There was a question in his tone.

My thoughts snapped to Val's purse, still hidden in the drawer of the bedside table in my room. "Yes," I said, perking up. "As a matter of fact, I did. Are you free to meet me at the resort? Or maybe I can get a ride over to the station."

"I'm nearby," he replied in his deep voice. "I can be there in fifteen minutes."

Perfect. I gave Detective Ray the number for Emma's and my room and hurried down the hall. My guilt over my spat with Noa was temporarily forgotten, replaced by excitement. Between turning over Val's purse and showing Ray the creepy photos taken by her stalker, surely he'd see that I didn't belong on his suspect list.

"Emma," I called as I stepped inside the room. "Are you here?" Silence was the only answer. I flipped on the light and felt my body go numb with shock.

It looked as if a tornado had touched down in our suite. Both Emma's and my suitcases were flipped upside down. Our clothes were strewn about the floor. Each of the comforters lay in crumpled heaps at the foot of the beds, and the flower arrangement I'd ordered for Em had been knocked over, the water from the vase dribbling down one leg of the coffee table and seeping into the carpet.

A gentle breeze wafted toward me, drawing my attention to the double doors that led to the private lanai. One of the sliding glass panes was ajar, and the curtains billowed as another draft blew in. In a haze of confusion and fear, I took a shaky step further into the room. Someone had trashed the place, but why? What were they looking for?

The answer struck me like a bolt of lightning, and my gaze flew to the little dresser beside my bed. The bottom drawer was open just a crack. *Please no,* I thought, rushing over to it. I dropped to my knees and yanked the drawer all the way open, feeling the breath leave my lungs as I stared down at the empty chamber.

Valentina's purse was gone.

CHAPTER FOURTEEN

———

"So, you're telling me that you had evidence, but someone broke in here and stole it?" Detective Ray stared at me from under furrowed brows. Though his tone was even, his rigid posture suggested that he wasn't happy. "What was it that you had?"

I gulped. *This isn't your fault,* I reassured myself. *It's not like you staged the break-in.* "Valentina Cruz's purse," I said, trying to keep my nervousness out of my tone. "Gabby LeClair called this morning to return what she thought was my bag, which had been left on the bus Friday night—but, as it turns out, it actually belonged to Val. I think that's why my purse was with her when she died. She must have mixed up the two and grabbed mine off the shuttle by mistake." I swallowed again. "But someone stole hers out my room."

"Did you go through the contents of the purse?" The detective's lips formed a firm line.

I flinched. "I took a peek, just to determine whose bag it actually was," I said, which wasn't entirely a lie. "There was quite a lot of cash in her wallet." I sucked in a breath. "And there was a receipt in there for a home pregnancy test." I hadn't wanted to tell him about the test, hoping he'd find the receipt himself when he examined the contents of the purse. However, considering the bag had been stolen, I didn't have much of a choice.

If the news shocked the detective, his stoic expression didn't show it. "Let me get this straight," he said, folding his arms over his broad chest. "You had possession of a purse belonging to a murder victim, and you riffled through it, getting your fingerprints all over its contents?"

Well, when you put it that way... I grimaced.

"So, you've contaminated potential evidence, which is now missing," he continued, his mouth drawing down in a frown.

I suddenly felt queasy. I'd wiped my prints off of her wallet but not the other contents I'd examined. All thoughts of covering my tracks had flown out the window at the sight of the drugstore receipt. From the detective's perspective, I'd just hampered his investigation.

"I was just trying to help," I said quietly.

Detective Ray sighed. "Next time you happen to stumble upon potential evidence, please call me before you touch anything." He gave me a pointed look.

"Of course," I said quickly.

He shifted his weight from one foot to the other. "While I'm here, I do have a question for you," he said, eying me closely. The suspicion in his voice was hard to miss.

I felt my mouth go dry. *He still thinks I might have done it, doesn't he?* "What would you like to know?" I asked, forcing an even tone.

He flipped to a new page in his little notepad. "Can you tell me why your hair was found on the victim's body?"

My blood chilled. "I, er, don't know," I replied shakily. I thought for a moment. "I guess Valentina must have used my hairbrush. It was in my purse."

"I see." He didn't sound convinced. He wrote something down in his notepad.

"Detective," I said to get his attention as something else occurred to me.

He looked up from his notepad with a look of forced patience. "Yes?"

"Was Val's phone found with her body?"

The question seemed to take him by surprise. "Her phone?" he repeated, his eyes narrowing slightly.

I nodded. "It wasn't in her purse," I explained, suddenly feeling sheepish. I didn't want to overstep my boundaries, but the fact that it had been missing from her bag was still nagging at me. I waited silently as Detective Ray studied me for a few more moments. Finally, he shook his head.

"Miss Cruz's phone was not found on her person," he said, still eying me warily. "But if you have any information as to its whereabouts, you should tell me."

"I don't," I said quickly.

"Very well." Ray glanced down at his notepad again. "Do you want to file a report?" he asked, using his free hand to gesture toward the mess.

I shook my head. "No. Aside from Val's bag, I don't think anything else is missing." Though I'd only done a cursory search through my scattered belongings, everything had appeared to be there. I'd called Emma to inform her of the break-in, but she hadn't answered her phone. My gut told me that none of her possessions would be missing either. It seemed that whoever had entered our room had been looking for the purse—but how had they known I'd had it? And why had they wanted it?

I mentally retraced my steps from the time I'd retrieved the bag from Gabby's Island Adventures to the moment I'd hidden it in the drawer of the little bedside dresser. Everyone in the wedding party had seen it. I'd had it with me at Loco Moco Café when I'd sat down with Bryan and all the other groomsmen. Bryan had even commented on the purse, hadn't he? *He'd thought that it was Valentina's.* Coco had also seemed to take notice of the bag when I'd returned to the room. Mia, Emma, and Dante had been there too—maybe one of them had also seen it. *But before that...* I'd bumped into Andrew Ryan on my way to our room, which had set off my whole afternoon of chaos. The thought of Val's stalker called forth another important memory: the pictures I'd found in his briefcase.

I met Detective Ray's gaze, trying to contain my excitement. "There's actually something else you need to see," I told him, pulling out my phone. I tapped at the screen, locating the photo I'd snapped in Andrew Ryan's room. I held it up to show him.

The detective looked puzzled as he glanced from me to the image on my phone. "What am I looking at, exactly?"

"A photo taken by Valentina Cruz's stalker," I said matter-of-factly. "His name is Andrew Ryan, and he's staying right here at the resort."

Once again, if this was news to Detective Ray, he gave no indication. "How did you get this photo?" he asked, frowning.

Uh-oh. If I told him that I'd sneaked into Andrew's room, he *really* wouldn't be happy.

Thankfully, the beep of a key card against the door scanner pulled his attention toward the room's entrance. Emma strolled in, followed by Dante. "Kaley, we just met those bakers you recommended. Their cake was to die for—" She stopped short, eyes going wide with alarm as she took in the disastrous state of our suite. "What happened?" she asked, her voice shrill.

Dante moved closer to his fiancée, slipping one beefy, protective arm around her. "Who did this?" he asked, looking from me to the detective.

"We don't know," I said, grimacing. "Someone broke in while I was out of the room with Jamie."

Emma's lips trembled. "Oh no," she whispered.

"None of Miss Ross's or Ms. Kalua's belongings appear to be missing," Detective Ray said, and I felt a smidge of relief that he didn't mention Val's purse.

Dante's expression grew stormy. "So someone just came in and trashed the place for no reason?" he asked skeptically.

Emma pulled out of his grasp. "Let me check just to be sure everything's here," she said, her voice frantic. "I brought several pieces of expensive jewelry with me—and my new wedding dress was in the closet." She blew out a shaky breath and set to the task of combing through her own scattered possessions. Dante joined her.

Detective Ray turned to me. "I expect you to send me that photo," he said in a low voice, "and then delete it from your phone." Though he didn't press me to reveal how I'd obtained the image, his stony expression told me that I'd better not let him catch me snooping around any other suspects' rooms or I'd really be in hot water.

"Of course," I agreed, instantly forwarding the image to his phone, though I didn't delete it as he'd instructed. *Just in case.*

"Nothing seems to be missing," Emma confirmed after a few minutes, her relief evident in her tone. Her face crumpled. "I just can't imagine why someone would sneak into our room and trash it," she said, her lower lip trembling. "I'm starting to think this trip is cursed."

"I'm sorry for all the trouble, Miss Ross," the detective said in a sympathetic tone. "Would *you* like to file a report? Kaley has already declined the option."

She frowned but shook her head. "No, I guess not, since nothing is missing. Thank you for your time, Detective."

Ray gave a polite nod before seeing himself out of the room. As soon as he was gone, Emma collapsed onto the bed. "Who would do something like this?" she asked, glancing helplessly at the mess.

I shook my head. "I don't know. The patio door was open. Maybe it was just some bored kids looking to get into some trouble." Though I hated lying to her, I hated even more the thought that she'd blame me if she knew the truth. I wasn't sure what Emma and Dante would think if they knew I'd hidden Val's purse in our room rather than giving it to Bryan or taking it straight to the police station.

Emma stared at the open glass door that led to the lanai. "I'm pretty sure I forgot to lock it when I was out there this morning," she said after a few moments. "I'm so sorry, Kaley. This is my fault." I tried to ignore the pang of guilt as I watched her begin to pick up her strewn clothing and place it back into her suitcase. Dante and I joined in, and within ten minutes, we had the suite looking back to normal.

"I'm going to take a shower," Emma said. She turned to Dante. "I need to get ready for the luau, but I'll head up to your room around six thirty." She glanced back at me. "Were you able to get tickets for the guys?"

"Yeah." I nodded. After a phone call where I'd pleaded with Juls Kekoa, she'd managed to scrounge up some extra tickets that were normally reserved for resort employees only. In return, I was going to let her take advantage of my manager's discount on her next shopping trip to Happy Hula. While resort employees received ten percent off their purchases, Happy Hula workers got double that deducted from our bill.

Emma gave me a small smile. "Thanks, Kaley. I knew I could count on you." She stood on tiptoe to give Dante a goodbye smooch on the cheek. "Bye, sweetie."

"See you later, boo," he said, squeezing her gently. He walked toward the door. As soon as Emma had disappeared into the bathroom, however, he turned around. "Kaley, we need to talk," he said quietly, his dark eyes boring into mine.

My stomach clenched. "Sure."

Dante crossed the room and sat down on the love seat just as the sound of running water came from the bathroom. I took a seat across the coffee table from him, folding myself into one of the chairs. "What's up?" I asked, trying not to sound as anxious as I felt.

Dante studied me through narrowed eyes for what felt like an eternity. "You're one of Emma's best friends," he began, his expression softening. "And she and I wouldn't be together if it weren't for you."

Uh-oh. "I sense a *but* coming," I said, feeling my chest tighten.

Dante met my gaze, his eyes hard. "Look, I'm not stupid. I know some little punk kids didn't break into your room. Did you have something to do with this?"

I winced but didn't respond.

Dante sighed. "It's nothing personal, Kaley. It's just..." He shot a furtive glance toward the bathroom door. "I'm worried about Em. She's going through a lot right now, and she doesn't need any more stress." He looked back at me. "So whatever's going on, just promise me you won't pull her into the middle of it. Please."

"I'm sorry," I said quietly. "I would never let anything happen to Emma. You know that."

Dante nodded curtly. "Good." He rose from the love seat and walked toward the door. "Be careful, Kaley." He stepped out into the hallway and closed the door behind him.

I stared after him, frowning. The blunt exchange with Dante had left me feeling a little raw—and at the same time, a little suspicious. There was no denying that he really cared about Emma, but his warning seemed rather ominous. Was it purely out of concern for his fiancée, or was there something more behind his words? Maybe he'd been trying to discourage me from looking for Valentina's killer. Could he be trying to protect someone? *His best man, Bryan—or his cousin, Coco, maybe?*

My phone dinged with a series of incoming texts from Jamie.

Sorry about earlier! How'd it go with Noa?

At my apartment getting ready for the luau, but I can jet back over if you need me.

A knot formed in my stomach at the memory of my fight with Noa.

Not great, I typed back. *Might need you to bring ice cream. Or wine. Lots of wine.*

Another message from Jamie popped up.

Ouch. That bad, huh? I'll be there in fifteen.

I scrolled through my contacts until I landed on Noa's number. It had been nearly an hour and a half since I'd left an apology on his voice mail, and he still hadn't returned my call. I stared at the screen for a few moments, silently psyching myself up. *Just call him back and tell him you're sorry.* I nervously pressed the *Send* button, sucking in a painful breath as it went to voice mail after the first ring. I didn't leave a message this time. Noa would call me back when he was ready. *I hope.*

Feeling dejected, I made my way over to the closet mirror and distracted myself with combing the tangles out of my long hair and freshening my makeup. I'd just finished touching up my lip gloss when my phone rang and Jamie's name popped up on the screen. "You almost here?" I asked as I answered.

"Kaley," Jamie practically hissed, her tone low and urgent.

A knot began to form in my stomach. "What's wrong?"

"I left my watch in my work cubby at the boutique, so I dropped by on the way to your room. I was just passing back through the courtyard when I heard a commotion at the pool bar. Bryan and Coco are over there, and they're going at it. It's like a scene from a reality TV drama." Even as she spoke, I could hear shouting in the background.

The hair on my arms prickled. "What are they fighting about?"

"I'm not sure," she replied in that same hushed voice. "But she keeps calling him a liar." She gasped. "Coco just sloshed her drink in his face!"

"Yikes," I whispered.

"Jimmy Toki just showed up. He's separating them." Jamie was quiet for a few moments. "Bryan's storming off," she said finally. "Coco's not following. It looks like she's actually heading your way."

I glanced toward the door that connected my room to the adjacent one. "Hurry over. Let's try to talk to her and see what their fight was about."

"On my way," Jamie replied before hanging up.

About thirty seconds later, the door to the other room slammed so hard that it shook the wall. I could hear Coco fuming as she stomped around. Whatever she'd been arguing with Bryan about had left her pretty steamed.

The sound of running water cut off in the bathroom. "Is everything okay?" Emma called. "I thought I heard a door slam."

"It's fine," I replied. "I'm heading to Mia and Coco's room for a bit." I gently opened the door connecting the two rooms and found Coco sprawled across the bed, a box of tissues beside her. She lifted her head as I entered, and I saw the dark mascara stains trailing down her cheeks.

"What do *you* want?" she groused in between sniffles. Her head dropped back onto the pillow.

"I heard the door slam and wanted to make sure everything was okay," I said honestly.

"No, everything is *not* okay," she shrilled. There was a slur to her words. Coco was drunk. I might be able to use that to my advantage.

"I know I'm not your favorite person," I admitted. "But you look like you could use a friend." I sat down on the foot of her bed. "Wanna talk about it?" I offered.

Coco rolled over on the bed and grabbed the tissues. She brought one to her nose and blew loudly. I fought back a look of disgust as she flung the used Kleenex onto the floor. "Do you really want to talk with me about your stupid ex-husband?" she asked skeptically.

"If there's anyone who knows how much of a slimy jerk he can be, it's me," I replied dryly. "What did Bryan do now?"

Coco blinked at me through soggy eyes. Then she shook her head. "Men," she wailed before burying her face into the pillow.

"Knock, knock," came a soft voice. I turned around to find Jamie standing at the door that connected this room to the one that Emma and I were sharing. "Emma said you were in here. I brought the wine," she said, holding up a bottle of Merlot.

"Wine?" Coco sat up again and eagerly eyed the bottle.

I nodded. "You're not the only one with boy trouble," I told her. I grabbed the bottle and corkscrew from Jamie and then crossed the room to retrieve several plastic water cups from atop the small refrigerator. I poured three drinks, keeping one for myself and passing the others to Coco and Jamie. "Cheers," I said, tapping my cup against Coco's.

She took several big gulps. "Top it off," she slurred, holding out her cup. She watched me curiously. "What kind of boy trouble are you having?"

I sighed. Maybe if I was honest with her, she'd return the favor—especially if she was as drunk as she seemed. "I got into a big fight earlier with the guy I'm seeing. It was my fault," I admitted. "I called him and tried to apologize, but I haven't been able to get in touch with him."

"Sorry, girl," Jamie said, coming to stand beside me. As if reading my mind, she glanced at Coco. "What about you?" she asked, giving the drunk woman an empathetic smile.

Coco drained half her cup. "Men are liars," she spat. "All of them. First they tell you they want to be with you, and then they start dating your friend. And now—" Her words were cut off by a hiccup. Coco looked at me, and I could see the hurt and confusion in her teary eyes. "I saw Bryan on the beach the night that Val was killed," she blurted.

"You did?" I struggled to contain my excitement. My plan was working! The intoxicated woman was ready to confess what she knew.

Coco nodded guilty. "I followed them toward the beach from the resort bar. I didn't see what happened." She hiccupped again. "I lost sight of them, so I headed toward the pier." She took a sip of wine. "I ran into Bryan when I was heading back toward the courtyard. He wanted to know why I was out there, and I admitted that I'd been looking for him." She wiped at her eyes with the back of her hand and then looked at me with a hurt expression. "I just had to know why he chose Val over me. She was terrible to him, always nagging and pouting when she didn't get her way. I would have treated him so much better." Coco sighed. "Bryan told me we should save our talk for when I wasn't so drunk. He walked me back to the courtyard and told me to go sleep it off."

"Wow. Bryan was actually a gentleman?" I couldn't hide my skepticism.

The blonde woman glared at me. "Can I finish my story?"

"Of course." I gestured for her to go ahead.

Coco sighed. Her lips began to tremble. "When I heard that Val's body had been found on the beach the next day, I freaked. I'd seen Bryan go out there with her and then come back alone." She hung her head guiltily. "But I covered for him. I didn't tell the police that I'd seen him out there." She swallowed. "I know it was wrong, but I thought maybe if I protected him, he'd finally see how much I care. But when I confronted him about it at the pool bar just now, he acted like he didn't know what I was talking about. He denied that he was ever on the beach that night." Tears rolled down her cheeks. "He said I was just a crazy, desperate drunk."

I stared at the crying woman for a few moments. Coco was too intoxicated to be lying, wasn't she? If so, maybe I could get more information out of her. "I'm sorry he treated you so horribly," I said gently, exchanging a glance with Jamie. "You saw Valentina and Bryan arguing at The Lava Pot before they went out to the beach, didn't you?"

She bobbed her head.

"Do you know what they were fighting about?" I pressed. "Could Val have been keeping something from Bryan, maybe?"

"Val was full of secrets," Coco muttered bitterly.

My pulse quickened. "What kind of secrets?" I asked, leaning forward eagerly.

Coco finished her wine and tossed the cup on the floor. "I think I need to sleep this off," she said, stifling a yawn. She sloppily waved a hand toward Jamie. "Thanks for the booze."

"You're welcome." Jamie nodded. "Always happy to dish out the liquid therapy."

Coco rested her head back against the pillow. Within seconds, she was snoring softly.

"So much for that," I muttered, picking up her discarded cup. Jamie and I tossed our own cups into the trash can before sneaking quietly out into the hall.

"So, she passed out before she could tell us the scoop about Val," Jamie said, shrugging. "Big whoop. The real bombshell is that she saw Bryan go to the beach with Valentina before she was killed—and then she covered for him. So he doesn't have a real alibi after all, assuming Coco's telling the truth." Her forehead wrinkled. "Think she was telling the truth?"

"I think she's too drunk not to be," I replied. "So, yeah— it sounds like Bryan's alibi is a bust." Of course, the only person who could corroborate Coco's story was my ex himself, and I doubted he'd be as forthcoming with the information as she had been. Still, it was enough to bump him higher on my suspect list.

"What about Andrew Ryan?" Jamie asked. "Did you find anything in his room?"

"Oh!" I snapped my fingers. I hadn't told her about the pictures I'd found in his closet. I quickly caught her up to speed. "I don't know who seems guiltier," I told her. "Andrew or Bryan."

"We could try confronting this stalker guy face-to-face," Jamie suggested. "Why don't we head back up to his room right now? We've got time to kill before the luau."

I blinked at her. "I already broke in once. Do you think it's a good idea to return to the scene of the crime?"

She shrugged. "Hey, there's safety in numbers, right? We'll go in together."

I thought briefly of Detective Ray's warning that I should stay out of his investigation, along with Noa's plea that I not go looking for trouble. Jamie *was* right, though—I'd have her along with me. If Andrew Ryan turned out to be dangerous, he couldn't hurt us both. Could he? "Okay," I said, slinging my tote bag over my shoulder and starting down the hall. "Let's do this."

CHAPTER FIFTEEN

———

"I'll knock," Jamie said a few minutes later as we stood at the door to Andrew Ryan's room. "If he sees you at the door, he might not open it, but maybe he won't recognize me."

"Good point." I moved aside to give her some room.

She lifted her hand to knock but then hesitated. Her expression turned thoughtful. "It couldn't hurt to throw on a little disguise, just in case." Jamie retrieved a turquoise scarf from her purse and pulled it over her sandy hair, tying it below her chin. Then she took a pair of tortoiseshell-framed glasses out of a little black case and perched them on the bridge of her nose.

I stared at her. "I didn't know you wore glasses."

"Just for reading," she said with a shrug. "Do you still have Andrew's wallet?" She held out her hand so that I could drop the leather billfold into it. Opening it up, she took out a twenty-dollar bill and stuffed it into her cleavage. "Trust me," she said when I started to protest. Jamie stepped forward and lightly tapped her knuckles on the door.

"Just a minute," called a voice on the other side. I heard the sound of heavy footfalls approaching the door. It swung open, and Andrew Ryan poked his chubby face through the threshold, his eyes fixed on Jamie. An oily smile curved his mouth. "Are you the girl from the dating app?" he asked in a husky voice, his gaze lowering to Jamie's tight-fitting halter top. "You look a lot different than your picture online—not that I'm complaining."

I bit back a groan of revulsion. *He's been trolling the internet for hookups.*

"Actually, I came to return this." Jamie held up his wallet.

"Hey!" Andrew looked from the billfold to my friend, his eyes narrowing. "Where did you find that?"

"Down at the pool," I said, stepping forward. "You must have dropped it when you were running away from me earlier."

The man's eyes snapped to me, and his expression soured. He made a move to grab the wallet from Jamie's hand, but she yanked it back.

"Nuh-uh. Not so fast," she said, dangling it out of his reach. "We'll return the wallet if you'll answer a few questions for us. Mind if we come in?"

A vein throbbed in his forehead as he glared at us. Finally, he nodded. "Okay, fine. But only for a few minutes. I'm expecting company."

"Right. The girl from the internet," I said dryly. That won me another glare.

Mr. Ryan stepped back and allowed us to follow him into the room. I glanced toward the closet on my way past, shuddering as I recalled the folders filled with images of Valentina. Was the man just a harmless Peeping Tom, or did he have more sinister intentions? We were about to find out.

In the hours since I'd escaped from Andrew's room unnoticed, he'd managed to undo all of the housekeeper's hard work. Clothes were strewn across the bed and love seat, much like the mess I'd come back to in my own room—though I didn't get the impression that the man had encountered any other intruders.

Andrew mumbled something under his breath as he grabbed a crumpled T-shirt and his orange swim trunks off the love seat and motioned for Jamie and me to sit. He pulled the little desk chair away from the wall and set it down on the opposite side of the coffee table so he was facing us. "What do you want to know?" he demanded gruffly.

"Did you attack me in the sauna this afternoon?" I asked bluntly.

The man's eyebrows rose. "Sauna? What sauna?"

"The one in the resort spa," I replied. "Someone blocked the doorway and then turned up the heat. Seems like they wanted me to burn."

"Jeez," he said with a snort. "That sounds brutal. Who'd you piss off, lady?"

"That's what I'm trying to find out." I narrowed my eyes at him. "If you had nothing to do with it, why were you watching me so intensely at the pool right after I escaped?"

A pervy grin spread across his round face. "Really? A hot chick like you, wearing nothing but a towel, lunges out onto the patio, and you want to know why I was staring?" His smile widened. "I was hoping the towel would slip."

My stomach lurched with disgust. *Pig.*

"Then why did you run?" Jamie asked.

He shrugged. "I thought maybe that guy with the dreadlocks was your boyfriend," he said, meeting my gaze. "I didn't want to get beat up for checking out some other guy's woman right in front of him."

I pursed my lips. Had he really thought Freddy was my boyfriend, or was he lying? It was hard to tell. I wasn't sure how much longer he'd cooperate, so I decided to cut to the chase. "Why are you in Aloha Lagoon, Mr. Ryan?"

"Why does anybody come here?" he asked in a tone of mock innocence. "I'm on vacation."

"So, you just happened to show up in Hawaii at the same time that Valentina Cruz was here? That's a pretty huge coincidence, considering you'd been stalking her for weeks," I challenged, crossing my arms over my chest.

Andrew blinked. "You think I was stalking Miss Cruz?" For a moment, he looked genuinely taken aback. Then he smiled, his green eyes twinkling with amusement. "Okay, so I'm a stalker now." he said, chuckling to himself. "That's a new one."

"I *know* you were," I said angrily. "And I can prove it." I rose from the couch and stormed across the room, heading straight for the closet.

"Hey, what are you doing?" Andrew protested, and I heard footsteps as he got up to follow me.

I flung open the closet door and snatched the briefcase from the floor, flipping it open before he reached me. "These are proof," I said, grabbing the top folder and holding it up. "There are dozens of pictures of Val in here. You've been following her every move."

"Of course I was following her." Andrew shot me a dark look as he wrestled the briefcase away from me. "I was being paid to do it."

"Huh?" I blinked at him.

He carried the briefcase across the room and set it down on the coffee table. I followed, returning to my seat next to Jamie just as he retrieved something from the bottom of the pile of folders. I felt my jaw go slack as he held it up for us to see.

"You're a PI?" Jamie asked, her tone disbelieving.

"Yep." Andrew handed her the private investigator's license so she could give it a closer inspection.

"Then why wasn't this card in your wallet?" she asked accusingly.

He shrugged. "Didn't need it. My mark is dead. That means until I pick up another client, I'm off the clock." He grinned and folded his hands behind his head. "Like I said before, I'm on vacation."

I leaned over Jamie's shoulder, bewildered as I stared down at the license. "Why would a PI need to follow Valentina around?" I asked, unable to hide my confusion. "And why fly all the way across the country to do it?"

"I was hired to," he replied in a huff. "Her boyfriend paid me to keep tabs on her. He thought she was running around on him."

My gaze snapped back to the sleazy investigator. "*Bryan* paid you to spy on Val?"

"So much for client privacy," Jamie remarked.

Andrew blew out a breath. "Whatever. I already told all of this to the cops. Colfax paid me two grand a week to follow the girl around and take a few pictures. He was convinced she had a secret sugar daddy back in Atlanta."

There may have been a daddy, all right, I thought, picturing the drugstore receipt again. I thought back to the money in Valentina's wallet. It suddenly seemed much more significant. Had the cash come from someone other than Bryan? Maybe Val had come clean about the pregnancy to her other lover, and he'd paid her a little premature child support. *Or hush money.*

"What did you find out?" I asked quietly as Jamie handed the license back to him.

Andrew shrugged. "Nothing. The only guy I ever saw her with was Bryan himself."

"Then why did he keep paying you?" Jamie pressed, her brow furrowed.

"Good question," I added, suspicion crawling up my back as I looked at the PI. "Bryan doesn't like to waste money." If he'd given my ex the proof he'd needed that Val wasn't being unfaithful, then why was he still on his payroll?

The man gave me a greasy smile. "I told him my findings were inclusive," he said in a sly tone. "I know what he does for a living. Pro athletes rake in a lot of dough, and I figured there's no harm padding my own little nest egg as long as he's willing to shell out the cash." He snorted. "Not that it matters, anyway. The guy is dead convinced that Valentina was cheating. He didn't even trust her to be loyal on this trip, even with him staying at the same resort. He paid for my ticket and booked me a room just so I could keep an extra close eye on her." Andrew shook his head. "Seems to me he's got some major trust issues."

Well, isn't that ironic? I thought sourly. I pushed aside my bitterness at Bryan's own infidelities and focused on the important information the greedy investigator had just divulged. Had Bryan thought that Val would hook up with some random islander, or did he suspect that one of Dante's other groomsmen might be the other man? If something had happened to prove his suspicions true, could he have killed Valentina in a jealous rage? What if he'd planned to murder her all along and had paid for Andrew Ryan to come to Hawaii so that he could take the fall? I had to be sure I could count the PI out as a suspect before I jumped to such a dark conclusion.

"Where were you early Friday morning when Valentina was killed?" I asked, carefully studying his face. "I know you followed us to the Lanai Lounge—Jamie saw you—but what about after? Did you follow Val to the beach?"

The man shook his head. "Nah. I tailed you ladies back to the resort, but my stakeout ended when I saw the girl meet up with Bryan at that little tiki bar."

"The Lava Pot?" Jamie supplied.

He nodded. "After that I came upstairs and ordered a little room service, if you know what I mean." He winked, his lips curling in a leer that made my skin crawl. A knock sounded at the door, and he rubbed his hands together. "Speaking of which, I'm afraid our time is up, ladies. I have a guest."

I reached for the stack of pictures on the coffee table and picked up the one on top. It was similar to the image I'd captured on my phone earlier that afternoon, though it was taken from a slightly different angle. In this one, Val and Bryan were walking toward the parking deck next to his high-rise condo. There was something about the picture that bothered me. The couple's backs were to the camera, and they were walking several feet apart. Even from far away I could see the stiffness in Bryan's posture. He seemed angry.

"Can I keep this one?" I asked as Jamie and I rose from the love seat and followed Andrew toward the door.

He paused and turned around to face me, a greedy glint in his eye. "Sure. For twenty bucks." When I glowered at him, he added, "I'm going to need some cash for my date, after all."

I grudgingly reached into the depths of my tote and fumbled around for a moment before I remembered that my wallet was probably in an evidence locker at the police station by now. All I had was my backup credit card, and I wasn't about to ask this slimeball if he took plastic.

Fortunately, Jamie stepped forward, reaching into her halter top to retrieve the bill she'd taken from the man's wallet. She handed it over to the sleazy private investigator. "You can pay me back later, Kaley," she said, winking when the man wasn't looking.

"It's been a pleasure, ladies," Andrew said, his voice dripping with sarcasm. He opened the door and stepped aside to let us pass. A young woman in a tight, silky black dress was standing in the hallway, using the camera function of her smartphone to check her lipstick. She backed up a few steps as we emerged from the room. Jamie leaned close and whispered something to her. The woman's freshly glossed lips formed a surprised *O* before her face crinkled in a look of disgust. She muttered something to Andrew and then turned to stalk off in the opposite direction.

"Hey, wait! Where are you going?" he demanded, scurrying after her.

Jamie and I continued on our way silently down the hall. When we reached the elevator, I turned to her and arched a curious eyebrow. "What did you say to that woman?"

She smirked. "I suggested that she steer clear of our crusty friend unless she wanted to catch a nasty case of crabs."

We both dissolved into a fit of giggles as the elevator doors slid closed.

"Now what?" Jamie asked when the laughing subsided.

My smile faded. "I don't know," I said quietly. "Nearly everything we've learned points to Bryan, but something is still bothering me." I looked up at her. "I wish I knew what happened to Valentina's phone. It wasn't in her purse when I picked it up from Gabby's office earlier, and Detective Ray admitted that the police don't have it, either."

"Do you think it could still be out on the beach?" Jamie asked. "Maybe she dropped it in the sand."

"Maybe," I said, frowning. "But I'd think the police would have found it, unless it was buried pretty deep." I looked up at her. "Maybe the killer has it."

"We could try calling it," she suggested. "Do you know her number?"

I shook my head. "I'm sure Detective Ray already tried that, too. The battery must be dead. I'm not an expert, but I don't think most carriers can locate a dead phone." I shrugged.

"What good would it do to find it?" she asked.

I thought for a moment. "Well, if Bryan *is* innocent, the real murderer could have lured Val out to the beach with a call or a text." An idea began to take shape in my mind. "Say that, hypothetically, her phone is still out on the beach somewhere. If I can find it and charge the battery, I could see if any calls or texts came in on late Thursday night or early Friday morning." Or maybe I could find out who she'd been texting from the Lanai Lounge.

Jamie grinned. "I sense a plan forming."

I winked. "You know me too well." The elevator dinged, and the doors slid open. We stepped off onto the first floor. I glanced around to ensure no one was close enough to hear us. "Tonight, during the luau, I'm going to sneak out to the area where Val's body was found and see if I can find that missing phone."

"How can I help?" Jamie asked. "Want me to be the lookout?"

"No. I'll need you to cover for me at the luau in case anyone is looking for me. There's no sense in us both getting into trouble if we're caught breaching the crime scene." I met her gaze. "But there is one thing you can help me with."

"Name it."

"Do you know where I can find a metal detector?" I smiled. "I think it's time for a little treasure hunt."

CHAPTER SIXTEEN

———

"Aloha to all our guests and friends." The emcee's voice boomed from the speakers by the stage. It was an hour and a half later, and Jamie and I were seated at our reserved table on the Ramada Pier with the rest of the wedding party. I zoned out as the host continued the same rehearsed greeting speech that he delivered during each luau, instead studying the faces of the others seated at the table.

Tom was sitting quietly at the opposite end of the table. Next to him, Freddy and Will were whispering to each other as they checked out a pair of hula dancers dressed in traditional grass skirts. Will caught me watching them and winked at me before turning his attention back to the hip-shaking beauties. Mia was playing with her phone, sneaking occasional glances at Will.

Emma was snuggled up to Dante, nestled under the crook of his arm as she watched the welcoming ceremony. I shifted my gaze to Coco. She was looking down at her cup of rum punch with a forlorn look on her face. Though she'd tried to cover them with too much makeup, her eyes were still puffy from her crying fit earlier that afternoon. As I watched, the scorned woman glanced across the table at Bryan, and her expression grew even more pained.

I followed her gaze, focusing on my ex-husband. He was staring straight ahead, his eyes glazed over as if he were lost in thought. I couldn't help but wonder if perhaps Coco had been telling the truth about her run-in with Bryan on the beach. According to her, he claimed it never happened. Was he trying to cover up what he'd done, assuming that the police would think Coco was lying to save her own skin? *Is she just throwing him under the bus now to get back at him for rejecting her?* From personal experience, I knew they were both liars and cheats—but which one was the guilty party this time around?

After meeting with Andrew Ryan and learning of Bryan's jealousy-fueled decision to hire an investigator to stalk Val on his behalf, I was leaning toward him as the culprit. *And yet...* I frowned. There was still something about the whole thing that just didn't quite add up. Hopefully my plan to sneak away and search for Valentina's phone would prove fruitful. If there was a possibility that Bryan was innocent, the evidence might be in the dead woman's texts or call logs.

I clapped along with the rest of the luau guests as the emcee finished his welcome speech. Resort employees dressed in traditional Hawaiian garb marched between the tables, some banging drums and others carrying large platters piled high with food. Once the dishes were arranged on the large buffet, guests began filing toward the table to fill their plates. When it was my turn, I helped myself to some pineapple fried rice, vegetables, and poi, though the nervous anticipation of my little mission was having an adverse effect on my appetite. Once we were seated again, I absently poked at my rice as I listened to the others chatter about the food and entertainment.

The hula dancers shimmied their way in between the tables, playfully encouraging the men to get up and dance with them. I watched as several dancers coaxed Dante, Freddy, and Tom up onto the stage to learn how to hula.

"Can we talk?" I looked up, startled to find Bryan standing over me. I hadn't noticed that he'd risen from the other side of the table.

I studied him for a few moments, suspicion brewing. Why would he want to talk to me? It was possible that Bryan was falling back into old habits, looking for me to comfort him after the great loss he'd suffered. Or maybe he knew what I'd been up to and was hoping to determine just how much I'd learned about the true identity of Valentina's murderer. Either way, with Tom preoccupied up on the stage, he couldn't prevent us from speaking. Perhaps I could use this opportunity to my own advantage.

"Sure," I said, gesturing to the empty chair beside me. Out of the corner of my eye, I caught Coco watching us, her teeth clenched. I met her gaze, and she shot me a withering look before rising from her own chair and storming over to the buffet for a refill of rum punch. *Is she jealous?* Our conversation earlier in her room had given me the impression that she was through with Bryan, but perhaps that wasn't the case after all.

Bryan sat down and then turned in his chair so that he was facing me. With his blond hair, piercing blue eyes, and blue and white aloha shirt, he looked like a Hawaiian Tourist Ken doll. "I know things are strained between us after everything I put you through," he said, his tone sincere. "And I realize that I never said I'm sorry." He exhaled. "So, I guess I'm doing that now."

I blinked at him. I certainly hadn't been expecting that. "That's very big of you," I replied, unable to hide my surprise. "Thank you."

"Kaley, can I ask you something?"

I nodded slowly and a little reluctantly, unsure of where this was going.

Bryan dropped his gaze down to his hands. "When we were together, was I a bit overbearing?" An unmistakable current of guilt ran through his tone, and I suddenly realized that this conversation probably wasn't just about me.

"You could be a little jealous at times," I said, downplaying the truth a bit. "And possessive—but deep down, I always thought you trusted me." I looked him in the face. "I mean, it's not like you hired a private investigator to follow me around and watch my every move."

The color drained from Bryan's face. "You know about Andrew," he said, his voice so low that I had to strain to hear him above the steel drum music coming from the stage.

"I had a little run-in with him earlier today," I admitted. "But from what I gather, you had nothing to worry about. He never caught Val cheating on you."

"So he claims," Bryan muttered, and his expression grew stony. He seemed to catch himself and shook his head as if to clear it. "Sorry," he said, the guilt returning to his voice. "I put up this big front when I'm around the team and the media, but you know that I can be insecure about stuff." He grimaced. "I just couldn't shake the feeling that she was hiding something from me, and I was hoping the PI could find out what that was. Val figured out what was going on when she spotted him following you girls around the nightclub on Friday night—she'd seen him around Atlanta a few times and recognized him. She confronted me about it in that little tiki bar, and we had a huge fight." He dropped his gaze to the table. "The last thing I ever said to her was that I couldn't trust her." He heaved a sigh. "That's going to haunt me for the rest of my life."

"I'm sorry, Bry," I said, and I meant it. I couldn't help but think of my own spiteful words to Noa before I'd stormed off earlier that morning. If something were to happen to him, I'd never be able to forgive myself for leaving things the way I had. *Focus, Kaley,* I reminded myself, shoving my own guilt aside. "What happened after you and Val left The Lava Pot?" I asked Bryan, carefully studying his face.

His forehead puckered. "I said good night and then went back up to my room to crash for the night. I'd assumed that she'd done the same until..." He trailed off, avoiding my gaze.

I glanced around the table. Jamie was playing around on her phone. Mia was flirting with Will, playfully running a hand over his close-cropped blond hair. Emma was seated with her back to us as she watched Dante and the other guys dancing on stage. Coco still hadn't returned to the table. No one was paying us any mind.

I looked back at Bryan. "So you didn't go out to the beach with Val?"

He shook his head. "No. I was back in my room by two thirty." He must have seen the skepticism in my face because his shoulders stiffened. "Why are you asking so many questions?" He frowned.

I decided to be up front with him. "I heard about your argument with Coco at the pool bar earlier—"

"And you believe that lying skank over me?" he demanded, his voice growing louder. "Jeez, Kaley. After all we've been through."

"After all we've been through?" I laughed humorlessly. "Bryan, you broke our wedding vows. I don't even know how many times you lied to me when we were together. Why should I take you at your word now?"

Mia and Will abruptly stopped talking and turned to stare curiously at us from across the table. So did Emma. I took a calming breath and forced it back out, struggling to rein in my temper. "Look," I said, lowering my voice. "I'm just telling you what I heard."

Bryan scowled. "Well, she needs to stop telling people that," he replied angrily, "before she lands me in hot water. I was never out on the beach that night. I already told the police that." He glared, his blue eyes boring holes through me. "And if you're going to throw around accusations, why don't you ask Emma where she and Dante were during that time? They weren't upstairs when I came back from The Lava Pot." His eyes narrowed to slits. "Maybe the precious bride-to-be is a killer, but I don't see you giving her the third degree."

I felt my face go slack. I looked from Bryan to Emma. Her face had gone as white as a sheet. "How could you say something like that?" she asked Bryan, the hurt in her voice unmistakable. Before he could respond, she rose from the table and hurried away, tears streaming down her cheeks.

"Emma, wait!" Mia got up and scurried after her.

Bryan whirled to face me. "Great. Now look what you did," he said gruffly.

"Me?" I scoffed. "That was all you, buddy." I began to stand up from my chair, intent on checking on Emma before I made my own exit from the luau, but Bryan reached out and grasped my arm.

"Tell me you believe I didn't hurt Val," he said. The anger had drained from his face, replaced by a look of pained desperation. "Kaley, please."

"Hey!" I let out a sharp cry when he tightened his grip. "Let go. You're hurting me."

"Whoa!" Will jumped up from his seat and sprinted around to our side of the table. "Bryan, what are you doing, man? Let her go." He grabbed Bryan's free arm and wrenched it back. "You're causing a scene," he said, his voice so low that I had to strain to hear it over the music. "There are tons of people here. Do you want some tourist's video clip of you having a meltdown to go viral?"

I glanced around the nearby tables. Sure enough, several heads had already turned our way.

Bryan grunted and released his grip on me. The tension seeped out of his body, and he sagged in his chair. "Sorry," he muttered. "I got carried away."

"Are you okay, Kaley?" Jamie asked, moving her chair closer to mine.

I gave a shaky nod. "I think I'm going to take a walk."

"Want me to go with you?" Will offered.

I forced a smile. "Thanks, but I think I just want to be alone. I need to clear my head." I rose from my seat and turned my back to Bryan, slipping between the other tables as I made my way back toward the resort.

Jamie caught up to me after a few steps. "Are you sure you're all right?" she asked, her face tight with worry. "That was intense."

"Yeah. I'll be okay. Just a little shaken up." I glanced back at our table, where Will had taken my empty seat next to Bryan. Their heads were bowed low in conversation. "Keep an eye on Bry," I said.

Jamie nodded. "On it." She turned and headed back to the table as I continued on my way.

When I reached the edge of the pier, I exhaled a long sigh of relief. My knees trembled slightly as I pictured the wild look on Bryan's face when he'd grabbed me. I didn't know what to make of his actions—had he really been that upset that I might believe Coco's version of events, or had he been worried that I might figure out that he was guilty? Never in all our years together had Bryan ever laid a hand on me. The action was certainly out of character for him, and it had rattled me more than I wanted to admit out loud.

I was also having trouble making sense of his accusation against Emma. Had she and Dante really not been up in his suite that night like she'd claimed? Why would she lie about that? Still, Emma hadn't exactly denied Bryan's claim. *And the look on her face*, I thought as I waited for my heart rate to return to normal. There'd been something in her eyes that I couldn't quite identify. Guilt? Worry?

And what about Dante's cryptic warning before? He'd made it clear that he didn't want me to cause any more trouble for Emma—could it be that the engaged couple was hiding something, too? And if so, what? I couldn't think of any reason that either Dante or Emma would want to harm Valentina, but suddenly I wasn't so sure that I could rule them out. It seemed the deeper I went, the more suspects I had. Nearly everyone in the wedding party had something to hide, and I was running out of people I could trust.

The sun had already set, and the shore was dark as I stepped onto the rapidly cooling sand. I reached into my tote bag and produced a small flashlight. Using the beam to illuminate my path, I made my way around the railing of the boardwalk to a row of dunes that were off limits to the resort guests.

"Thank you, Jamie," I said, grinning as I spotted the metal detector nestled in the saw grass on the first dune. While I'd been getting ready for the luau, she'd driven to a nearby beach equipment rental store. I quickly scooped up the metal detector and aimed my flashlight in the direction of the area where Valentina's body had been found.

The beach was mostly deserted at this time of night, with the majority of guests either attending the luau or enjoying dinner at one of the various restaurants on or near the resort. I turned off my flashlight and crouched low in the dark as another orb of light moved along the shore a few yards away. I heard the sounds of a young couple talking and giggling flirtatiously as they enjoyed a moonlight stroll. When the voices faded out of earshot, I turned my light back on and continued on my way.

I listened to the waves slapping the shore as I walked quietly through the sand, following the bouncing beam of my flashlight. After a few minutes, the yellow tape that marked the crime scene came into view. Goosebumps pricked my arms as I pictured Valentina's corpse sprawled beneath that same patch of sand. If her phone was still down there, I hoped I could find it.

Here goes nothing. I reached for the power switch on the metal detector. The device hummed to life, and I anxiously waved it over the sand in front of me. A static buzzing emanated from the device as I paced slowly across the small patch of beach, scanning the area just outside the yellow tape. A stronger signal sounded from the detector, and I dropped to my knees, digging excitedly in the sand. A few moments later, I sighed in disappointment when I unearthed a set of car keys.

I stood and dusted myself off before resuming my search, pushing the metal detector underneath the police tape. The device signaled once more that there was something beneath the surface. I set it down and crouched low, using my hands to shovel the sand to the side. I was so focused on my digging that I didn't hear my attacker approaching until it was too late.

I had only a second's warning as a spray of sand pelted me from behind. Then the air left my lungs in a sudden *whoosh* as someone shoved me down onto the beach. I cried out in surprise, my flashlight flying out of my grip as I toppled over. It landed several feet away, illuminating a small patch of the shore. "Hey!" I protested, struggling to roll over and face my assailant. Before I could move, something hard struck the back of my head with such force that my teeth nearly shattered. Blinding pain sang through me, and my vision blurred as I plunged into darkness.

CHAPTER SEVENTEEN

———

The distant rush of the waves roused me. The sound was muffled by the ringing in my ears, and my head felt as if the back had caved in. Carefully, I cracked an eye open, immediately closing it again when fresh agony flared. I took a shaky breath and tried again. This time I was greeted by a bright white light. *I'm dead*, I thought groggily. Another wave of pain rolled through me. *And this feels like hell.*

"Kaley?" Though the voice was also muffled, I was sure I recognized it. I waited for my eyes to adjust. Jamie slowly came into focus before abruptly disappearing behind the flashlight beam she was shining in my face.

"Hey, watch where you point that thing," I muttered, lifting a hand to shield my eyes.

Jamie exhaled. "Oh, thank God," she breathed, sounding relieved. "For a minute there, I thought you might be dead. I was about two seconds away from giving you mouth-to-mouth."

"I'm okay," I said hoarsely. "I think." I tried to sit up, but Jamie placed a firm hand on my shoulder to stop me.

"You shouldn't move," she instructed. "I had to complete some medical training as part of my diving instructor certification. It's important that you lie still until we determine that you don't have a neck or spinal injury."

"I don't think anything's broken," I told her. "And we already know I can move my arms." I sucked in a ragged breath and forced it back out. Then I closed my eyes and concentrated on my toes, feeling the sand shift beneath me as I wiggled them. Everything seemed to be in working order. "I think I'm okay." I reached up and gingerly rubbed at the large bump on the back of my head. *Ouch.* "Except for the fact that my brain feels like it's going to explode," I added, wincing. "What happened?"

Jamie frowned. "When you didn't return to the luau, I came looking for you. I'm pretty sure someone whacked you on the head with the metal detector. It's a miracle they didn't crack your skull." Her brow creased. "I really should call the paramedics. You could have a concussion."

"Don't," I pleaded. "If you call an ambulance, the police will probably show up too—and then I'll have to explain why I was out here digging through their crime scene." I grimaced. "I don't feel like spending the night behind bars."

"I don't know," Jamie said, her tone uncertain. "You could really be hurt, Kaley."

"I'll live," I insisted. "I just wish I knew who to thank for this migraine," I added dryly. "Did you see anyone else from the wedding party leave the luau after I did?"

"Well…" Jamie's tone was guilty. "I got a little distracted." Her gaze dropped to her hands. "Javi called. He wants to take me out again soon." She met my gaze, and even in the dim light I could see the remorse in her expression. "I stepped away from the table for, like, five minutes—ten, tops. I'm so sorry, Kaley. This is my fault."

"No, it's not." I tried to sound reassuring. "Was anyone still at our table when you came back? Will? Freddy? Mia?"

She frowned. "Just Dante. Emma never came back after Bryan upset her, and Mia left with her. Dante said that Will took Bryan on a walk to try to cool him off. I'm not sure where Freddy and Tom were, and I haven't seen Coco since she stormed off during dinner."

I sighed. "So my attacker could have been practically anyone."

"Pretty much," Jamie agreed.

"Great." I bit back a groan. Bryan had been really upset with me when I'd left the luau. He easily could have blown off Will and come looking for me on his own. Or maybe Coco had watched and waited until I left alone and had followed me out to the beach. She'd obviously been ticked that I was speaking to Bryan after she drunkenly poured her heart out to Jamie and me about how he'd spurned her. Even Mia could have come looking for me, angry that I'd provoked Bryan into upsetting Emma—or hell, maybe Emma herself, wanting to get back at me for making

Bryan expose her false alibi. Once again I found myself taking two steps back in my progress. I wasn't any closer to determining who was behind all this foul play.

"If you're not going to let me send for an ambulance then at least let me call Noa," Jamie said, eying me nervously. "He'll kill me if he finds out you were hurt on my watch."

"No!" I protested. As badly as I wanted to see him, I couldn't let him know I'd put myself in harm's way again. That, and I wasn't even sure if he was still speaking to me. "Leave him out of this," I pleaded. "I promise I'm fine. I just need some aspirin." *A whole bottle of it. And make it extra-strength.*

Jamie chewed her lip. "Okay," she said after a few moments. "But at the very least, you have to let me call Rikki."

I sucked in a breath. I wasn't sure which would be worse: dealing with my worried not-quite-boyfriend or my worried aunt. "How about option C?" I suggested. "We leave them both out of this, and you can stay at the resort with Emma and me tonight to make sure I'm okay. If I'm dead in the morning, you can say I told you so."

Jamie shook her head, but in the moonlight I could see the smile slowly spread over her face. "At least your sense of humor is still intact," she said wryly. "Deal. Come on—let's get out of here before someone catches us." Her grin faded. "Think you can walk?"

With her help, I slowly climbed to my feet. Then I took a couple of wobbly steps through the sand. "Yeah, I'll manage."

Jamie slung my bag over her shoulder and then grabbed the metal detector. Using her free arm, she helped me slowly make my way back to the boardwalk. I could hear the sounds of the luau still in full swing over on the pier as we turned toward the courtyard. By the time we reached the room, my migraine had lessened to a splitting headache. I slipped off my shoes and immediately sank down onto the bed without changing out of my dress.

Jamie dug around in her purse and retrieved a bottle of aspirin. She dumped two of the little pills into my palm and then handed me a glass of water. "Let me get you a cold compress, too," she offered. She grabbed the ice bucket from atop the mini fridge and disappeared out into the hallway for a few minutes.

When she returned, she wrapped some of the ice cubes in a hand towel and gave it to me.

"Thanks." I winced at the pain as I gently pressed it to the goose egg that had formed on the back of my head. Within a minute or two, the cold numbed the pain and made my existence a bit more bearable. I pulled the towel away from the wound and held it up for a closer inspection. "No blood, at least." I touched the compress to the bump on my noggin again and frowned at Jamie. "This has got to end."

"So you're giving up?" Jamie studied me from under twin, furrowed eyebrows. "Maybe it's for the best. This is starting to get dangerous."

I shook my head. "No. I can't just sit around and wait for Detective Ray to decide he wants to charge me with the crime. When I saw him this afternoon, he still seemed to suspect me. He found some of my hair on Val's corpse." I met her gaze. "So, I can't give up—but I also can't go chasing after the killer all alone. I still need your help, if you're up for it."

Jamie sat down next to me on the bed. "What do you think we should do?"

I was relieved that she was sticking by me. "I haven't figured it out yet," I admitted. A yawn escaped me, and I settled back onto the pillows and closed my eyes. "Maybe a good night's sleep will clear my head. We can start fresh tomorrow."

* * *

The next thing I knew, Jamie was shaking me awake. "Get up, sleepyhead," she chirped in her annoying morning-person voice. "The shuttle will be here to take us to the marina in half an hour."

I sat up groggily and blinked at her. She was dressed in aqua board shorts, and her metallic green bikini straps were peeking out from underneath her purple halter top. She must have gone back to her apartment at some point to grab fresh clothes. "How long have you been awake?" I mumbled.

She shrugged. "Long enough to head home, knock out a quick three-mile run, shower, and drop by the Blue Manu Coffee House for a couple of your favorites." She held out a brown paper bag and a Styrofoam cup. "One Kona brew and a macadamia scone. Oh, but first—" She pulled the food away just as I reached for it. "You should probably take some more aspirin." Jamie gestured to the two little pills and glass of water she'd already laid out for me on the bedside table.

"Thanks, Nurse Jamie." I quickly popped the aspirin into my mouth and chased it with the water.

"How are you feeling?" She gave me a concerned look.

"A little better," I answered honestly. The pain hurricane in my head had downgraded to a tropical depression.

Jamie studied me for a few seconds and then nodded, seemingly satisfied. "Good," she said, handing me the coffee cup and the paper bag. "Well, eat up. The food and caffeine will help you feel even better, and you're going to need all the energy you can muster when we're out on the water."

I smiled to show my gratitude and then closed my eyes as I took a sip of the rich Kona brew. "Have I told you lately that I love you?"

"Are you talking to me or the coffee?" Jamie grinned.

"Both." I took another sip and then pulled the lid off the cup so that I could dip my scone into the hot liquid.

"By the way," Jamie said, gesturing to the bedside table. "You might want to check your phone."

"Huh?" Brow furrowed, I set my breakfast down and reached for my cell phone. My heart fluttered as I noted the three calls I'd missed from Noa this morning. A moment later, it nearly stopped beating altogether. Though he hadn't left any voice mails, he had sent one text message containing four of the most dreaded words in the English language:

We need to talk.

"That can't be good," I groaned. I held up the phone so that Jamie could see and watched her expression fall as she read the screen.

"I'm sure everything's fine," she said, though she sounded uncertain. "Maybe he wants to accept your apology for yesterday in person. Or he could even want to apologize himself for being kind of flaky lately."

I sighed. "You don't send the we-need-to-talk text unless you've got bad news." I swallowed the lump in my throat and blinked a few times, warding off the tears threatening to form behind my eyes.

"Good morning," Emma called as she pushed the bathroom door open and stepped out. She was dressed in a canary yellow tankini and had her hair wrapped in a towel. If she was still upset about the events at the luau last night, she didn't let it show. "Your turn, Kaley," she said, pointing to the shower.

Feeling miserable, I grabbed the macadamia scone and took another huge bite before grudgingly rising from the bed. I slunk into the bathroom without a word.

"What's wrong with her?" I heard Emma ask Jamie as I closed the door behind me.

I turned on the water, fretting over Noa's cryptic text. Perhaps I really had pushed him a little too far the day before. If he wanted to hit the brakes on what was happening between us, I supposed I couldn't really blame him. Things had been going so well up until the past week—so of course I had to be a complete jerk and mess it up.

Even though it was all my fault, I indulged in a little self-pity as I washed my hair, careful not to irritate the whelp on the back of my head. Then I toweled myself off and pushed Noa out of my mind. I'd call him back after our snorkeling excursion and set up a time that we could meet so he could drop the ax in person. Until then, I would focus what little energy I had on drawing a confession out of Valentina's killer today on the boat. When we were out on the water, he or she would have no place to run.

CHAPTER EIGHTEEN

———

"All aboard," Jamie called thirty minutes later as we stood outside the main entrance to the resort. The wedding party began filing onto the same shuttle that we'd rented from Gabby's Island Adventures on Thursday night. Koma was our driver again, and he gave me a friendly nod as I stepped onto the bus. "I'm glad you were able to get your purse back, Kaley."

"Wait a minute." Coco, who was boarding the bus in front of me, turned around. She took off her dark sunglasses and looked at me, eyes narrowed in confusion. "Wasn't your purse found with Val—"

"Coco!" Jamie cut in, coming to my rescue. She scooted past me and ushered the other woman toward one of the seats. "How's that hangover treating you? I've got some aspirin and a bottle of water in my bag if you need it."

"I could really use that," she said wearily. "I got a little carried away with that rum punch at the luau last night." She sank down into the seat and pulled her sunglasses back over her eyes.

I smiled at Jamie as she sneaked me a quick thumbs-up. The front row of seats was still open, so I slid in and then turned around to survey the rest of the group. Bryan and Tom took the back row, with Dante and Emma in front of them. Bryan caught my gaze and quickly looked away. He'd been avoiding me since our little group had met in the lobby. Perhaps he felt guilty about his outburst at the luau. *Or maybe his guilt is over something else—like whopping me over the back of the head with a metal detector,* I thought. He'd let his true, violent colors show when he'd grabbed me as I'd tried to leave the table, so it was less of a stretch now to picture him trying to hurt me again. *Or hurt Valentina.*

Freddy grabbed a row to himself across from Will, who was cuddled up next to Mia. In front of them, Coco was slumped in her seat, her face twisted in a look of hangover misery. As I watched, she reached over with one hand to gingerly rub her other shoulder.

"What's wrong with your arm?" Mia asked from behind her.

"I think I slept on it wrong," Coco said, giving a little groan as she continued to massage her shoulder.

"Or maybe she pulled a muscle when she whacked you in the head last night," Jamie whispered as she slipped into the seat beside me.

"Yeah, maybe," I agreed, still frowning over my shoulder at the bleached blonde bridesmaid.

As Koma pulled the little bus away from the resort, I turned to stare out the window. A short drive later, we arrived at the Aloha Lagoon Marina. The dock was lined with dozens of sailboats, speedboats, and other small water vehicles. We filed off the bus and followed Jamie toward a medium-sized vessel docked near the far end of the port. The word *Ariel* was painted in red across the side of the boat. I wouldn't have expected anything less from my mermaid-obsessed friend.

"Isn't she a beaut?" Jamie said, grinning. "My favorite sea maiden."

I nodded. "Hey, isn't that Javi?" I asked as I spotted the tall, bald man waving to us from on board the boat.

Jamie gave me a sheepish look. "Emma said it was all right if he joined us. I hope you don't mind."

"Not at all." I smiled at her.

When we reached the edge of the dock, Javi held out his hand to help me on board the *Ariel*. "Hi, Kaley," he said warmly. "How's Noa? I was hoping I could convince him to hit the waves with me sometime next week."

My heart clenched at the mention of Noa. "He's fine," I said, forcing an even tone. Though Javi wasn't the type to pry, I didn't want him to know we'd hit a rocky patch. "I'll ask him to call you when I see him."

"Cool." Javi smiled at me before turning his attention to Jamie. His grin widened. "Hey there, beautiful." He helped her onto the boat, and I couldn't help but notice that his hand lingered on the small of her back for just a moment. "Thanks for letting me tag along."

"Glad you could make it." Jamie tucked her chin, and a rosy color appeared in her cheeks. *She really likes him*, I thought, pleased that my two friends were hitting it off.

Once everyone was on board, Jamie distributed life jackets and then took the helm, piloting the boat away from the marina. I took a seat on one of the cushioned benches and settled back against the railing, relishing the feel of the cool sea air on my face. It reminded me of the trips I'd taken out on the water with my parents and Aunt Rikki as a child.

After twenty minutes, Jamie slowed the boat to a stop. She and Javi set about dropping the anchor. The early morning sunlight shimmered across the water.

"How far out are we?" Freddy asked from beside me.

I squinted in the direction of the shore and could just make out a few tiny buildings in the distance. "Probably a few miles from land," I guessed.

"For those of you who aren't strong swimmers, I've brought several boogie boards," Jamie said, holding one up. "Feel free to grab one of these and use it to float on. The water's really clear today, so it'll be easy to peek below the surface with your goggles and check out some of the gorgeous marine life." Jamie placed the board back on top of the stack at the rear of the boat and then went about distributing snorkeling gear to everyone.

Once they'd donned their fins and goggles, Jamie and Javi climbed down into the water and beckoned for the rest of us to follow.

"This is going to be so dope," I heard Freddy exclaim to Tom as he fastened the rubber flippers to his feet. He pulled his dreadlocks back with a hair band then slipped his goggles over his face before waddling over to the edge of the boat. Freddy climbed over the side, and there was a loud splash as he hit the water. Tom followed.

Dante started to climb in after them but turned at the last minute, his gaze resting on Emma. "Are you coming, boo?"

Emma gave him a pained smile and then shook her head. "Not just yet. I'm feeling a little queasy." She grimaced. "I think I might be seasick."

Dante took off his goggles. "Then I'll stay with you." He took a few steps toward her, but I held up a hand to stop him.

"No, you go ahead, Dante," I told him. "I'll stay with her. I'm not feeling so great myself." If I was being honest, that bump on my head was still making me a little woozier than I cared to admit. Fighting the currents might not be the best idea right now. I forced a smile. "Plus I can go snorkeling out here anytime."

"Are you sure?" Dante looked from Emma to me, his brow furrowed.

"Of course," I insisted. "Go on and enjoy yourself."

Emma nodded. "Have fun, honey."

Dante reluctantly put his goggles back on before returning to the ladder.

"Thanks for that," Emma whispered to me as he disappeared over the side of the boat. "I'd hate for him to miss out on all the fun just because I'm..." She trailed off, her forehead puckered. "Under the weather," she finished.

I scooted closer to her on the bench. "Em, is everything all right? I know the stress of the wedding and what happened to Val have been a lot to bear, but I can't help but feel like there's something else you've been keeping from me." After Bryan's revelation that Emma and Dante hadn't been in the upstairs suite when he'd returned after his spat with Valentina, it seemed clear to me that my friend was harboring a secret.

Emma looked away. "Kaley, I wish I could talk to you about it—really." She grimaced. "But I just can't."

"We used to tell each other everything, Em." I studied her, not sure what reaction I was looking for.

She dropped her gaze to the deck. "Just trust me. Please?"

I wasn't sure what to say. I glanced over at Bryan, who was slipping his feet into a pair of blue fins. Will and Mia sat to his left, and Coco was on the other side of Mia. I watched the petite blonde stand up and cross the boat, peeking warily over the side. She reluctantly grabbed one of the boogie boards and then climbed onto the ladder, muttering about not wanting to get her hair wet.

Bryan stepped over to the side of the boat next, poised to descend the ladder. My gaze flitted to his back, and I froze.

"Is that a no?" Emma asked, noticing when I stiffened beside her. "You don't trust me?" She sounded hurt.

"What?" I jerked my head back toward her. "No, it's not that. Excuse me for a sec." I rose from the bench and retrieved my tote bag. I'd left the photos I'd taken from Andrew the PI back in our room at the resort, but there were still images on my phone from my time spent hiding in his closet. I pulled out my cell and flipped through the photos, noting the Atlanta Falcons tattoo just inside the right shoulder blade of the man walking beside Valentina. My gaze moved between my ex-husband and the image on my screen. Bryan's back was entirely ink-free, just as it had been when we were married. *That* was what had been bothering me before.

This isn't Bryan in these photos. Perhaps Val really had been cheating on him—which would give Bryan a motive for her murder.

"Hey, Will. Want me to help you put on some sunscreen?" Mia's voice broke through my thoughts. I looked up to find her batting her eyelashes at him in a flirty manner as she held up a blue bottle of SPF 50.

He shrugged. "Sure." I watched as Will tugged his black tank over his head and then turned around to allow Mia to slather the lotion on his back. I gasped loudly.

"How long have you had that tattoo?" I asked him, unable to keep the tremble from my voice.

He twisted around to look at me. "A couple of months," he said. "I got it to celebrate the end of my physical therapy." Will must have seen the shocked look on my face, because his own expression clouded. "Kaley, what's wrong?"

I swallowed the lump forming in my throat. "How long had you and Valentina been sleeping together?" I asked, loud enough that Bryan could hear. "Did you kill her so she wouldn't come clean about it to Bryan?"

Bryan froze on the ladder, his head snapping toward Will. "What?" he demanded, beginning to climb back onto the boat.

Will placed his hands in the air in a show of surrender. "Whoa. I don't know what you're talking about," he protested, though I could plainly see the guilt creeping over his face. "I—"

He didn't have a chance to finish his sentence. There was an angry cry from behind him, and Mia launched her sunscreen bottle at Bryan's face. It slammed into his forehead with a loud *smack*. Startled, Bryan let go of the ladder and tumbled backward off the boat. There was a loud splash, followed by the startled cries of the others already in the water.

I whirled around to face Mia in time to see her lunging for me, her arms outstretched and her face twisted with rage. "Leave Will alone!" she shrieked, clawing at my face with her hands. I ducked out of her way and rolled across the deck, but she was on top of me before I could get back on my feet. "I won't let you ruin him like Val tried to," she growled, pulling at my hair.

"What is going on?" Emma demanded shrilly. She started toward us, but Mia lashed out at her. I managed to yank the taller woman back just before she could shove Emma to the ground. Em stumbled backward, arms wrapped protectively around her stomach. "My baby," she cried. A look of wild anger flashed across her face. "You could've hurt my baby."

Shock zinged through me, and even Mia froze. We both whipped our heads around in unison, gawking at Emma as her words sunk in.

"You're pregnant?" I gasped.

Emma nodded, her eyes brimming with tears as she clutched her middle section.

Will used the distraction as an opportunity to seize Mia by the arms. "I'm not going to let you hurt anyone else," he said gruffly, dragging her away from me.

Mia screamed in protest, kicking and writhing in his grasp. "But I did it for you!" she wailed. Her foot connected with his groin, and Will's face turned red. He grunted in pain and released his grip on the struggling woman.

Mia broke away from him and lurched toward me again. "You couldn't just leave it alone," she growled as I shrank away from her. "You had to keep snooping around, sticking your nose in everyone's business." She glowered. "I should have hit you hard enough to kill you last night on the beach."

I rolled out of the way again as she dove for me, but Mia caught my left foot and tried to pull me back. Looking around wildly for a weapon, I spotted the blue bottle of sunscreen she'd thrown at Bryan. It lay on the deck just a few feet away, the cap open and white lotion leaking out onto the floor. I kicked Mia's arm as hard as I could with my free foot, and she let go long enough for me to inch my way toward the bottle. I grabbed it and twisted around to face her, aiming the plastic container at her face as I squeezed it for all it was worth. A stream of sunscreen hit Mia square in the eyes.

She howled in pain and dropped back, pawing at her face. "I'm going to kill you!" she screamed, lunging blindly toward me. I moved out of the way, and she careened into the side of the boat with a loud *thud*. Her body went rigid, and she slumped to the floor, unmoving.

CHAPTER NINETEEN

———

Will and I made sure that Mia was still breathing, but we were careful not to move her since we weren't sure how serious her injuries were. He volunteered to stand guard over her, and I tended to Emma as the others climbed back aboard the boat. Em was clearly distressed after Mia tried to shove her, concerned for the well-being of her unborn child.

"Is that what you couldn't tell me?" I whispered as I gingerly helped her over to one of the benches.

She nodded, tears streaming down her face. "It's still so early. We haven't even been to the doctor yet to confirm it." She swallowed. "I only just found out myself on Wednesday night."

My jaw went slack as my mind began to connect several dots. "Was that *your* receipt for a home pregnancy test from Peachtree Drugs?"

Her hazel eyes grew large. "How did you know about that?"

"I retrieved Valentina's purse from Gabby's Island Adventures yesterday, and I found the receipt inside."

Emma shook her head sadly. "I ran into the drugstore after I picked up Val on the way to the airport Wednesday night. I thought I'd tossed the receipt on the floorboard of my car, but it must have landed in her bag." She closed her eyes. "I wonder if she noticed it."

"Emma!" Dante rushed over to his fiancée. "Are you all right?" he demanded. "What happened?"

She smiled weakly. "I'm okay, thanks to Kaley. She stopped Mia from hurting me." She lowered her voice. "She knows about the baby."

Dante's brows reached for his hairline. "How?"

I shook my head. "It doesn't matter. Your secret is safe with me." I glanced over my shoulder at Will, who was crouched next to Mia's prone form, his expression stoic. "Will knows too, but I think he's got enough of his own to deal with. I doubt he'll be telling anyone."

"What happened up here?" Dante asked, looking from Emma to me.

Freddy appeared at his side looking equally confused. "Who pushed Bryan into the water?"

Jamie kneeled next to Mia for a few moments, checking her pulse. "We need to get her to a doctor," she said grimly. "I'll radio for help. What happened to her?"

Emma and I recounted the details of Mia's meltdown, and all eyes turned toward Will.

"Did you sleep with my girl?" Bryan accused angrily. He was seated on the floor with his back resting against the bench. There was a small gash oozing blood from the center of his forehead, but it didn't look deep enough to require stitches.

Will vehemently shook his head. "No, man. Nothing like that." His shoulders slumped. "She was blackmailing me."

"So, you killed her?" Tom asked, his hands balling into fists. He started toward the other man, but I called out to stop him.

"It was Mia." I looked to Will. "Wasn't it?"

He nodded slowly, though guilt showed on his narrow face. I studied the young kicker closely. I'd never noticed it before, but with his short, sandy hair and newly muscled physique, at a glance, he really did look a lot like Bryan. No wonder Andrew Ryan had thought it was Bryan in all the photos he'd taken of Valentina. If it hadn't been for the tattoo, I wouldn't have realized it wasn't my ex, either.

Tom and Freddy both stepped toward Will, wearing matching looks of anger. "Start talking, Bolero," Tom said angrily.

Will sucked in a breath and forced it back out. "There was no way I was going to recover from my broken leg in time to get in shape for the season," he said quietly. "My girlfriend even dumped me because she thought my career was over." He laughed bitterly. "Jessica said she wasn't about to hitch her wagon to a fallen star. I thought she loved me, but she just wanted a piece of the fame—and my money." He sighed, and the muscles in his face strained. "I needed to heal faster, so I started juicing."

"Steroids?" I gaped at him. The sweet, charismatic Will that I'd known back in Atlanta never would have resorted to doping.

He hung his head. "It was only for a couple of months. I was desperate to get back in shape. The problem was that Val walked in on me shooting up. I thought I was alone in the locker room, but Val had sneaked in there looking for Bryan." He grimaced. "She snapped a photo of me on her phone and threatened to turn me in to Coach or leak it to ESPN if I didn't pay her. I thought it was a one-time deal, but she started demanding money every week."

I remembered the excess cash in Val's wallet. She hadn't had a sugar daddy like Andrew and Bryan had thought. She'd been extorting one of Bryan's teammates for the money.

"She texted me on Thursday night and told me to meet her on the beach when we got back to the resort," Will continued, hanging his head. "She wanted more cash for the weekend. I was fed up with her constantly squeezing me dry, and we argued. I didn't even know Mia had followed us out there until she launched herself at Val. She whacked her across the temple with a piece of driftwood. I tried to wake Val up, but she was dead."

"Why did Mia follow you?" Javi asked. I looked over to find that he'd slipped a comforting arm around Jamie's shoulders.

Will grimaced. "We hooked up once a few weeks ago back in Atlanta. I was still broken up over my ex, so I wasn't looking for anything serious, just a rebound—but Mia just wouldn't take the hint. She's been obsessed with me ever since." He cut a guilty look toward Bryan. "If I'd known she was crazy enough to kill someone, I never would've gone near her."

Bryan dropped his gaze to the ground. His shoulders began to tremble. "What happened next?" he asked without looking up. His voice was thick with emotion.

Will cleared his throat. "Mia threw the driftwood and Val's phone into the ocean and said that I had to cover for her.

She said if I didn't corroborate her story then she'd turn me in and tell the police that I'd done it."

"Why didn't you just tell Detective Ray the truth about her?" I asked.

Will flinched. "I panicked. My whole career was at stake." The color drained from his face. "And now I'm ruined." He sighed. "Mia had already told the cops that I'd been in her room and that we'd slept together, so I went along with it." He shot a look at Coco. "The only problem was that I ran into Coco on my way back from the beach that night."

"That was *you*?" Coco gawked at him. "I thought you were Bryan." She clasped a hand to her chest. "Jeez, how drunk was I?"

"Pretty hammered." Will ducked his head. "You kept calling me by Bryan's name, so I didn't correct you and just hoped you wouldn't realize your mistake when you sobered up."

Coco glared at him for a few moments. Then her face softened and she turned her gaze to Bryan. "I'm sorry I accused you of lying," she said quietly. "I thought you didn't appreciate that I was trying to protect you."

"By lying to the cops," Jamie muttered under her breath, though Coco didn't seem to hear her.

"Don't worry about it," Bryan said gruffly. He didn't look at her. His gaze was fixed on Will, the pain of his loss written plainly on his face.

"That's as far as it went for me," Will said, his voice pleading. "I swear. Mia's the one who locked Kaley in the sauna." He looked at me. "And she broke into your room to steal Valentina's purse so she could give me back the money Val had taken from me. She sneaked through the door that connected your rooms and then trashed the place to make it look like someone had broken in through the patio." He hung his head. "But I didn't ask her to do any of that. It was all her."

"You *did* have Val's purse?" Bryan eyed me suspiciously.

"Long story," I said, avoiding his gaze. There'd be time to explain that later. "Mia also attacked me on the beach last night," I told everyone. "She even admitted it. I think Will's telling the truth."

"But that still makes you an accomplice," Freddy said, scowling at Will. "How could you, man?"

Will sagged against the side of the boat. "Like I said, I panicked. I know I can't take any of it back, but I'm really sorry." He looked morosely around the rest of the group. "I'll turn myself in as soon as we get to shore."

Jamie climbed into the captain's seat. "An ambulance is meeting us at the marina," she said, "and so are the police." She started the engine and pointed the vessel in the direction of the Aloha Lagoon Marina.

We rode in silence most of the way back, everyone lost in their own thoughts after the dramatic turn the snorkeling trip had taken. When we were almost back to shore, I scooted closer to Emma. "How far along are you?" I asked, just loud enough so that only she could hear me over the boat motor.

Emma shook her head. "I'm not sure." She met my gaze, her features pinched with worry. "I just hope the baby's okay. With all the stress this weekend, and finding out that one of my closest friends is a murderer..." She trailed off, as if too horrified to finish the thought. "And it's so early in the pregnancy." Her eyes welled with tears. "What if something's wrong?"

"I'm sure he or she is going to be just fine," I said, trying to sound reassuring.

"Thanks." She squeezed my hand. "I'm sorry I caused you so much trouble when I ruined your alibi. I couldn't tell you the truth until I knew for sure, you know?" When I nodded my understanding, she exhaled a sigh of relief. "When you left the beach, I told Detective Ray about the pregnancy. I couldn't very well lie to the police." She swallowed. "I found out Wednesday night when I took that test and it came out positive. Of course, I wasn't entirely sure, so I had to keep it to myself. I didn't even tell Dante until I went up to his room early Friday morning when we got back from the nightclub."

I frowned. "But you were drinking all night, weren't you?"

A ghost of a smile played at her lips. "Nope. I wanted to play it safe, so I just pretended I was drinking. First, I pulled the server aside at dinner to make sure he brought me fruit juice instead of a cocktail, and then I went straight to the bartender at the nightclub and told him to do the same thing." Her eyes twinkled. "That double shot of tequila he served me was really just water."

"Sneaky." I grinned at her. "But smart." When I'd discovered the receipt for the pregnancy test in Valentina's purse, I'd suspected that she'd been the one pretending to be tipsy all evening. I'd never guessed that it had actually been Emma who was fooling us all along.

"Anyway, I couldn't take it anymore, so as soon as you fell asleep that night, I sneaked up to find Dante and told him about the pregnancy test. We had the concierge call us a cab and headed to the closest convenience store. I bought three more tests, and they all came out positive."

"That's great!" I slipped my arm around her shoulder in a half hug. "You and Dante are going to make incredible parents."

"Don't congratulate us yet," Dante said, leaning around Emma to meet my gaze. "It's still early, and Em's been through more than her fair share of distress over the past few days. I read online that it can be bad for the baby." He frowned. "As soon as we get to shore, I want to take her to see a doctor and make sure that everything is all right."

"Of course." I nodded. "Let me know if there's anything I can do."

He smiled sheepishly. "To start, you can accept my apology." Dante's eyes shone with sincerity. "I shouldn't have given you a hard time yesterday. You've always had Emma's back, and today you helped protect both her and our baby."

"And I'd do it again in a heartbeat," I said and meant it.

"I just can't believe Mia killed Val," Emma murmured. "I've known her since college, and she's always been such a sweetheart. A little boy crazy, yes, but I didn't think she had a malicious bone in her body."

Emphasis on the "crazy" part, I thought silently.

* * *

"I'd bet you money that her neck is broken," Jamie murmured twenty minutes later as we stood on solid ground again, watching a pair of EMTs push Mia on a gurney down the marina deck, toward a waiting ambulance.

"*Something's* definitely broken," I remarked, shuddering as I recalled the horrible sound of her head colliding with the side of the boat.

Just as promised, the police and an ambulance had been waiting for us when we'd arrived back at the marina. Awake but unable to move, Mia was carefully loaded onto the gurney with her neck wrapped in a protective foam collar. Her right wrist was also handcuffed to the cart, compliments of Detective Ray. As the EMTs tended to Mia, the homicide detective read her rights. He also took Will Bolero into custody. I watched sadly as the young kicker was led toward a waiting squad car, his head hung low and his hands cuffed behind his back.

"Hey, isn't that Noa?" Javi asked, commanding my attention.

I jerked my head in the direction he was pointing, and my heart skipped a beat. Noa was half-walking, half-running toward us down the deck. Our eyes met, and he broke into a full-on sprint.

"What are you doing here?" I asked as he reached us. He didn't answer, instead scooping me into his arms and lifting me off the ground. Noa pressed his lips to mine in a kiss so passionate it took my breath away.

"And hello to you too, Mr. Kahele," I heard Javi say in a joking tone, though his voice sounded far away.

After what may have been a tad too long to be appropriate in front of onlookers (not that I minded), Noa finally pried his mouth away from mine. "Don't say anything," he said, holding up a finger to my lips. Though he was still panting from his run and the kiss, his dark eyes were wide and serious. "I'm sorry I missed your calls and texts yesterday—my phone died while I was sitting on the patio at Loco Moco, working on my web design project. Look, Kales...I don't want to fight anymore. I'm sorry if I wasn't as excited about going to Emma's wedding as you wanted me to be, but I can explain. It had nothing to do with you." He dropped his gaze to the ground, a pained expression on his face. "Kaley, I'm deathly afraid of flying."

"You're what?" I sputtered, still a little dizzy from our kiss.

He grimaced. "I didn't know how to tell you. I'd never even left the islands until I flew to Los Angeles for that job several years ago. I was so terrified the whole flight that when I decided to move back to Hawaii, I couldn't even bring myself to buy a plane ticket." He met my gaze, his whole face tight with embarrassment. "So, I booked a cruise from LA to Kauai. Anything that wouldn't fit in my suitcase, I had shipped back through the postal service." He shuddered. "It cost an arm and a leg, but it was worth it not to be strapped into one of those flying death traps again."

I blinked at him. "That's it? Why didn't you just tell me?"

His shoulders slumped. "I didn't want you to think I was weak," he said, his vulnerability clear in his tone. He straightened up and took my hand in his. "But I don't want to lose you over something as stupid as my phobia of flying. And I want you to know that, if you'll still have me, I'd be honored to be your date to the wedding."

My lips twitched. "Oh, sure—you want to go now that it's here on the island," I teased.

He opened his mouth to protest, but I stood on tiptoe and planted another kiss on his lips. "How did you know I was here?" I asked when I pulled away.

Noa tucked his chin. "Jimmy Toki heard about the distress call from the boat on the police scanner in his office. He knew Jamie was taking the *Ariel* out today with some resort guests. He had a hunch that you were among the group, so he called me." His jaw clenched. "What happened out there?"

"I'll fill you in later," I said, squeezing his hand.

"So, this must be the infamous Noa," Emma said. I turned to find that she and Dante were standing behind us. Emma offered him her hand. "I've heard a lot about you," she said, grinning.

"Happy to finally meet you both. Congrats on the upcoming nuptials." Noa returned her smile and then shook hands with her fiancé.

Dante turned to Emma. "I should see if there's room for you in that ambulance," he said, gesturing to the vehicle carrying Mia.

"Why does she need to go to the hospital?" The question came from someone standing behind us.

I stiffened, turning slowly to face none other than Felicity Chase, annoying reporter extraordinaire. She must have seen the anger in my expression because she held up a hand to stop me from protesting her presence.

"I'm allowed to be here," she said, sweeping a hand around the dock. "This is a public marina. Not part of the resort property." She grinned. "And Mr. Toki's not the only one with a police scanner." She focused her attention back on Emma and Dante. "Mr. Becker, what's wrong with your bride?"

Emma shifted nervously, no doubt worried about how to get out of the conversation with the reporter without revealing the truth about her pregnancy. "I—" she stammered, but I cut in.

"She fell on the boat," I claimed, though my voice hitched slightly. I'd never been the best liar. I barreled through before the reporter had time to notice. "And I suggested that she go to the hospital and make sure she didn't sprain her ankle."

Felicity's gaze shot back to Emma, and I winked at Em over her shoulder.

"That's right," Emma said, playing along. She pointed to her left ankle. "It's not swollen, but I'm having trouble putting much pressure on it."

Felicity squinted at her, no doubt running the story through her internal bull-o-meter. "Are you sure that's all that's wrong?" she pressed, moving closer to Emma.

"Yep," I chimed in again. "You should let her get to the hospital for some x-rays. It'd be a shame if she weren't able to walk down the aisle tomorrow."

The reporter's eyes went wide. "You're getting married here on the island?" I could practically hear the potential headlines running through her mind. "A celebrity wedding," she murmured eagerly.

"You can come cover it, if you like," Dante offered. He shot a look at me over her shoulder. "Kaley will give you the details. Now if you'll excuse us, I'd like to get my fiancé some medical attention." He ushered Emma away before Felicity could get in another word. To Emma's credit, she limped quite convincingly all the way to the end of the dock before Dante scooped her up and carried her the rest of the way to the ambulance.

I grudgingly did as Dante instructed and gave Felicity the time and location for the ceremony.

"See you tomorrow!" she chirped excitedly before turning her attention to Detective Ray, who was huddled near a squad car with several uniformed officers.

I frowned after her as she chased down the homicide detective, probably begging for a quote about the arrests. *Better to let her cover the nuptials than to leak BabyGate across the internet*, I reasoned.

I shifted my gaze from the reporter to a trio standing at the opposite end of the deck. Bryan, Freddy, and Tom were huddled together, watching one of Detective Ray's men drive away in the car that held Will Bolero. Bryan caught me looking at him and made his way over to where we stood, the other two men at his heels.

"Kahele," he said by way of acknowledging Noa. I sucked in a breath and held it. It was the first time the two men had come face-to-face in over five years.

"Aloha, Colfax," Noa said gruffly. He wrapped an arm around me and pulled me closer.

Bryan seemed unfazed by the gesture. He met my gaze, his expression softening. "I just wanted to tell you I'm sorry," he said. "For how I've acted the past couple of days, I mean. I've been having a hard time coming to terms with what happened to Val, but I shouldn't have taken my grief out on you." He swallowed. "Thanks for uncovering the truth."

The Kaley Kalua Apology Tour continues. "You're welcome," I said evenly. "But I'm the one who should be saying sorry. I let my bitterness about our past cloud my judgment. I shouldn't have jumped to conclusions and assumed that you had something to do with her death."

"I can't really blame you," Bryan said. "But no harm, no foul. I'm just ready to put all of this behind me." He held out a hand to Noa. "Take care of her, man."

Noa nodded and shook his hand.

Bryan started to walk away, and Freddy followed. Tom paused long enough to give me a curt nod before joining them. It was an unspoken apology for the way he'd treated me over the past few days. I likely wouldn't get anything more from the big man, and that was fine by me.

* * *

Two days later, we all gathered for a gorgeous sunset ceremony on a cliff overlooking the ocean. Jamie stood next to me, twirling excitedly in her pink and teal bridesmaid dress and tan wedge sandals. A pink hibiscus was tucked behind her left ear. Coco and I wore outfits identical to hers—and, to my dismay, so did Harmony Kane. With Mia behind bars, Emma was down yet another bridesmaid, so she'd asked Harm to step in. Normally I'd have protested, but Harmony actually seemed excited about the opportunity—especially when she caught sight of Freddy Jenkins, who would be escorting her down the aisle. Considering Mia had almost cooked her to death in the sauna alongside me, I figured she deserved to be included.

The four of us stood in a row at the end of the sandy path that led to the cliff's edge where Emma and Dante would soon say their I-do's. The groomsmen were lined up on the opposite side of the path from us, wearing khaki shorts and matching teal and white aloha shirts. Dante had also been down one man, thanks to Will's involvement in Mia's crimes. He'd asked Noa to take his place, and Noa had graciously accepted.

Further down the path, local photographer Autumn Season was snapping photos of Dante as he viewed his bride for the first time on their wedding day. I was filled with a warm, happy sensation as I watched his face light up when he laid eyes on her.

Emma and Dante had met with a doctor at a local hospital to confirm that all was well with her pregnancy. Em was seven weeks along, and not only was the baby doing fine, but they were able to see an ultrasound and hear the heartbeat. The parents-to-be had been over the moon excited, and I'd been just as ecstatic—especially when Emma had pulled me aside first thing on the morning of her wedding and had asked me to be the godmother. I'd given her a very enthusiastic yes and had promised that until they were ready to share their baby news with the world, I'd keep their secret—even from Noa.

Dante squeezed Emma's hand and then left her to take his place next to Pastor Dan Presley at the cliffside so the ceremony could begin. Our sales associate, Rose, had agreed to hold up Noa's tablet so that the couples' parents could watch the nuptials via FaceTime. She took her place off to the side, next to the reception table with a three-tiered pineapple wedding cake, courtesy of local bakers, Liam and Ellen Bentley.

Pastor Dan gave a signal to Nani Johnson, and she began to strum "Somewhere Over the Rainbow" on her ukulele.

Emma had asked Aunt Rikki to give her away, and I watched the pair take their places at the end of the wedding procession line. Emma looked radiant in her white linen dress and pastel pink lei. My aunt winked at me as she slipped her arm through Em's and prepared for their entrance.

Two by two, the bridesmaids and groomsmen met at the top of the path and walked in pairs down to the cliff's edge. First went Jamie and Tom, followed by Harmony and Freddy. Though the best man and maid of honor were normally paired together, Emma and Dante had agreed to make an exception. That meant that Bryan walked with Coco, leaving Noa to escort yours truly down the aisle.

Possibly not for the last time, I thought as I walked toward him, grinning. Noa took my hand and squeezed, and my stomach filled with happy butterflies as we took our first step along the path to join the others. My little L-word slip up from the other day had been all but forgotten, but that didn't mean I wasn't open to the possibility that there could be wedding bells in our future…much farther down the road from now, of course. As for the present, I was content to just sit back and enjoy the ride.

ABOUT THE AUTHOR

USA Today bestselling author Anne Marie Stoddard used to work in radio, and it rocked! After studying Music Business at the University of Georgia, Anne Marie worked for several music venues, radio stations, and large festivals before trading in her backstage pass for a pen and paper (Okay, so she might have kept the pass...). Her debut novel, *Murder at Castle Rock*, was the winner of the 2012 AJC Decatur Book Festival & BookLogix Publishing Services, Inc. Writing Contest, and the 2013 Book Junkie's Choice Award Winner for Best Debut Fiction Novel. It was also a finalist for Best Mystery/Thriller in the 2014 RONE Awards.

Aside from all things music and books, Anne Marie loves college football, Starbucks iced coffee, red wine, and anything pumpkin-flavored. Anne Marie is currently hard at work on several books.

To learn more about Anne Marie, visit her online at:
http://amstoddardbooks.com

Visit the official

aloha lagoon

website!

Trouble in paradise...
Welcome to Aloha Lagoon, one of Hawaii's hidden treasures. A
little bit of tropical paradise nestled along the coast of Kauai, this
resort town boasts luxurious accommodation, friendly island
atmosphere...and only a slightly higher than normal murder rate.
While mysterious circumstances may be the norm on our corner
of the island, we're certain that our staff and Lagoon natives will
make your stay in Aloha Lagoon one you will never forget!

www.alohalagoonmysteries.com

If you enjoyed *Hanbags & Homicide*, be sure to pick up these other Aloha Lagoon Mysteries!